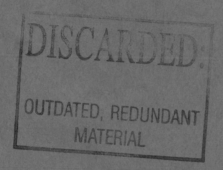

Sweet and Sunny

❀ ❀ ❀

Sweet and Sunny

COLEEN MURTAGH PARATORE

SCHOLASTIC PRESS / NEW YORK

Library of Congress Cataloging-in-Publication Data

Paratore, Coleen, 1958–
Sweet and Sunny / by Coleen Murtagh Paratore. — 1st ed.
p. cm.
Summary: Despite facing a host of problems, old and new, optimistic fourth-grader Sunny continues her quest to create a national Kid's Day and improve other holidays, especially the upcoming Valentine's Day, while bringing joy to those around her.

[1. Holidays — Fiction.   2. Valentine's Day — Fiction.
3. Self-confidence — Fiction.   4. Mothers and daughters — Fiction.
5. Schools — Fiction. 6. African Americans — Fiction.]   I. Title.
II. Title: Sunny Holiday number two.
PZ7.P2137Suf 2010
[Fic] — dc22   2009007162

ISBN: 978-0-545-07582-4

10 9 8 7 6 5 4 3 2 1   10 11 12 13 14

Printed in the U.S.A.   23
First edition, February 2010

The text type was set in Apollo MT.
Book design by Lillie Mear

To my beautiful goddaughter, Lauren Claire Murtagh,
and to all the little lions —

bloom, bloom, bloom

— C.M.P.

The snow is snowing
The wind is blowing
But I can weather the storm.
What do I care how much it may storm?
I've got my love to keep me warm.

— from "I've Got My Love to Keep Me Warm"
as recorded by Billie Holiday

Sweet and Sunny

❀ ❀ ❀

Contents

CHAPTER ONE

Holiday Girl

Everybody wants to be famous.

"Ain't you that holiday girl?" shouts a lady all bundled in blue as Jazzy and I pass the bus stop on our way to school.

I blush inside, warming up a bit, but I keep walking.

"*Uh-huh*. That's right," Jazzy says, stopping us, swagging her head all proud. She links my arm and pulls me in close to her. "This is my best girl, Sunny Holiday. You saw her on TV, didn't you? She was on every single channel, at six and eleven, too."

Folks huddled in the grimy plastic bus house turn to investigate. Two old women nod at us and talk, their words making Caspers in the February air. A puffy-cheeked baby swipes the ghosts with her mitten and giggles. A bone-skinny tired man on the bench leans closer to listen. There's a boy, sixteen maybe, in a summer-thin red sweatshirt. He studies my face, then pulls his red hood down over his forehead like a tent. He is not impressed.

"I knew it was you," the blue lady says all excited, coming toward us.

She probably recognizes me from my ugly green glasses; nothing else about me paints a picture you'd remember.

"You're the girl wants to make some kinda big

new holiday for kids. And the mayor promised you could do it. Ain't that so?"

Isn't that so, I think, but it would be rude to correct her grammar. That's a teacher's job.

The boy in the red tent pokes his head out. He's not wearing gloves. His hands must be frozen. His face has that slumped expression like so many brothers I know. There's a whole world of sad in his eyes.

"You *famous*?" he shouts loud to me.

"No," I say.

He ducks back into his tent and draws the flap down, *good night.*

"Yes, she is *too* famous," Jazzy says. "Sunny just got started last month and she's already been in all the newspapers and TV shows and . . ."

Oh, no, Jazzy, please stop talking. . . .

"And you know Candy Wrapper?" Jazzy keeps on going like that bunny on TV.

The boy nudges his hood up a bit, just his eyes peering out, and stares hard at us.

"That's right," Jazzy says, shaking her head up and down, hands on her hips. Everybody on the corner is paying attention now. "Ms. Candy Wrapper, the best girl rapper on the *planet* Candy Wrapper, called my girl Sunny last month from her fancy suite at the Crowne Plaza Hotel and sang a specially dedicated song just for Sunny right over the telephone."

The boy flips full out of his tent, *good morning*. "Yeah, right," he taunts, his sad eyes crinkling mean now. "And Kanye's coming to my house for dinner tonight. My mom's out buying steaks right now."

Two men on the bench elbow each other and chuckle. I pull Jazzy's arm. "Come on, Jazzy, we'll be late for school."

Jazzy plants her boots in the dirty snow, but I give her my serious face and she finally comes along.

"You *are* the holiday girl," Jazzy starts up again as we walk. "You *are* famous, Sunny Holiday. Don't be so humble. How many girls our age you know been on TV and go to lunch with the mayor in that mad cool black limousine and are first-name-friends with the best girl rapper on the . . ."

"Jazzy, *please.*"

"What's wrong with being famous, Sunny? Everybody wants to be famous. And you are, girl. You may not know it yet. But you are *famous.* And I'm your best friend so that makes me a little famous, too. Right?"

I laugh. She's got a point there. "Come on, Jazzy. *School.*"

CHAPTER TWO

The State Tests

Smartest, smartest, smartest.
Hmm, hmm, hmm, *that felt good.*

Mr. Otis, our never-smile principal, such a grump, is standing on the top step under the sign *New Hope School*, in a camel-colored coat with a matching hat and a red and black checked wool scarf.

"Ooh, fancy," Jazzy whispers. "Mr. Otis is stepping up his wardrobe."

"Maybe he's in love," I whisper back. "Could be he has a crush on a teacher or one of the lunch ladies."

Jazzy giggles, cupping her mitten over her mouth.

"Good morning, Mr. Otis," I shout up to him all cheery as we pass. I stare him straight in his eyes like always, trying to make him see me back.

He doesn't. Mr. Otis motions me and Jazzy along like he's a robot directing traffic, like he detects human voices, compute-compute, but he isn't programmed for eyes-to-eyes contact. Maybe that's just in the newer robot models.

"Move along, fourth graders," Mr. Otis says.

"Ooh," I say. "At least that's something."

"What?" Jazzy says.

"At least Mr. Otis knows we're in fourth grade.

Maybe by the time we graduate he'll even know our names."

"That's if they don't close us down first," Jazzy says.

Like I could forget. New Hope School is in trouble.

When our school first opened, there was a big party with balloons and a huge cake. Jazzy and I got our picture in the paper with the mayor cutting the welcome-in ribbon.

But now the party's over. Now it feels like a prison around here — work, work, work and rules, rules, rules and lots of no-smile serious speeches.

No one asked me, but I blame it on those stupid tests. You know the ones I'm talking about. Those big long *bor* . . . . . . *ing* tests they make us take every year to see which schools are good and which schools are bad, like Santa Claus making his list and checking it twice, gonna find out who's naughty or nice.

Well, New Hope keeps scoring at the bottom of the sea, worse than that, the bottom of the D. One more bad year and they'll fail us. And there's no summer school for schools.

At our opening assembly in September, Mr. Otis made a very long and loud no-smile serious scary speech, *welcome back*, about how this was "the do-or-die year" for New Hope and how the state tests in January would be the most important tests we'd ever take. The day was so hot and his speech was so long my butt nearly glued to the floor in the gym. Jazzy said her butt fell asleep.

Personally, I think Mr. Otis could have whipped up some more hopeful, encouraging, sparkly words to inspire us with — he had all summer to write that speech — but I'm not saying anything. He's the principal.

There's a glimmer of hope for New Hope, though. My and Jazzy's teacher, Mrs. Lullaby, she's the best, told us a secret.

Our whole class had been working so hard all through the fall doing practice tests and extra homework sheets and everything, getting ready for the real tests in January. Mrs. Lullaby kept telling us we were doing great and then, when our class took the final practice test right before the holiday break, guess what?

Mrs. Lullaby said we were the smartest fourth grade in the *whole state*!

Well, actually, she said we were *"among* the smartest fourth graders in the entire state," but all we heard was "smartest."

Smartest, smartest, smartest. *Hmm, hmm, hmm*, that felt good.

Mrs. Lullaby gave us each a roll of Smarties candy. "Smarties for my smarties," she said, her face shining like a teacher-apple. I was so proud I thought I would burst.

Mrs. Lullaby asked us to keep our smartness a secret, though, so we wouldn't make the other fourth grades feel bad. We promised we wouldn't brag.

The morning of the *real,* butterflies-in-our-tummies test a few weeks later, Mrs. Lullaby had a gigunda-munda bag of Smarties positioned on her desk, just waiting as a treat for when we finished. She never mentioned the candy, but we all saw it there, *sweet.*

When Mrs. Lullaby came around to our desks to collect our worries like she does every morning, she gave us each a brand-new number-two pencil with a fat yellow smiley-face eraser and an even-better Mrs. Lullaby smile, too.

After the pledge and the announcements, Mrs. Lullaby asked us to close our eyes and take some good deep breaths. Then she reminded us how "well prepared" we were, and how "smart" we were, and how "very proud" of us she was. I felt myself blooming like a dandelion in my chair. I couldn't wait to start.

Now, I can't speak for my classmates, and we haven't heard how we did yet — maybe Mrs. Lullaby will tell us today — but I must say . . . that was the easiest test I ever took.

And . . . I never boasted about Mrs. Lullaby's class being the smartest to the other fourth grades, no way, but I did let the secret out. I didn't plan to. It just slipped.

Shortly after we took that final practice test, Mayor Rockefeller Little the Third came to Riverview Towers apartments, where Jazzy and I live, to announce his re-election campaign. I went to the Community Room event, planning on asking him to make a holiday just for kids, something I'd been thinking about for a while — you know, like there's a Mother's Day and a Father's Day, what about Kid's Day? But when I got up in front of the room and took the microphone, all these other thoughts started spilling out, too, and before I knew it, I was asking the mayor why he never fixed the city pool that's been closed now for two scorching summers, and when was he going to clean up the litterbug rock wall and the muddy river, and what about that park with swings and slides he promised us when he first got elected and all we got was six droop-sorry trees instead . . . . . . and then everybody was cheering and clapping and Mayor Little's face was bulging big as a bag of popcorn in the microwave, I swear I thought his face might explode . . . and in the excitement of it all, I sort of got carried away with all of those TV cameras glaring at me and I bragged out Mrs. Lullaby's secret. *Oops.*

After my speech that night, Mayor Little named me Junior Deputy Mayor of Riverton, New York. Momma says someday I'll be president.

I have my own office down in the Community Room, and once a month the mayor sends his limousine to bring me to a lunch meeting with him at Jack's Oyster House so we can discuss important matters. I tell him what my neighbors are concerned about and I report on how plans are coming along for the first annual Kid's Day we'll be having next January. I'm holding my first committee meeting next week.

The way I imagine it . . . first Kid's Day is going to be a Riverton holiday . . . then a state holiday . . . then a national holiday . . . then someday the whole world will celebrate Kid's

Day — one extra-special day for children all around our spinning globe — all the cities, all the countries, all the continents. Happy Kid's Day. Happy Kid's Day. Happy Kid's Day. Hoorah!

First we've got a whole lot of planning to do, but I know one thing for certain already — Kid's Day is going to be *great. Can't wait!!*

CHAPTER THREE

"Where Is Mrs. Lullaby?"

She makes school more fun than summer.

Outside our classroom, Jazzy and I hang up our backpacks and lunch packs in our lockers. We take off our matching red coats and hats and mittens that came handed down from the Levy twins in 5-H. Jazzy and I are twins, too. Sister-twins. Different mommas, different birthdays, sister-twins just the same.

Jazzy and I giggle doing our one-foot-hop-hop-switch from our boots into our shoes. Crystal Lord and Davina Bishop, two of those snobby bus-girls, look over at us. We call them the bus-girls because they live in the nice houses up on Hill Street and take that banana yellow bus to school. The bus-girls think they are better than us because they've got more money. They are wrong.

"Babies," Crystal says, rolling her eyes at me and Jazzy. Crystal fixes her hair in the pink mirror in her locker that has heart stickers and boy faces taped all around.

"Like that sorry girl's gonna make a holiday," Davina says, sneering at me. They must have seen me on TV.

Jazzy starts singing one of Candy Wrapper's new songs real low and I hum in.

"*Ugh,*" Crystal says. "What do you sorry girls know? Davina and I were at Candy Wrapper's concert. We had tenth-row seats."

"Maybe so," Jazzy says, "but Ms. Wrapper herself called Sunny right at her house that night and sang her a song on the phone dedicated especially to 'Miss Sunny Holiday.'"

The bus-girls burst out laughing.

"Liar," Crystal says. "Candy Wrapper did not, no way."

"Yes way," Jazzy says. "Right, Sunny? Tell her."

Crystal slams her locker. "River rats," she throws at us over her shoulder, and she and Davina walk off laughing.

Why do those girls hate us? They are so lucky, living up in those pretty new houses with front porches and big backyards, taking that nice warm bus to school. They don't even need snow boots. Why can't they just be grateful for what they've got and stop always trying to make us feel small?

The bus-girls call me and Jazzy and the other kids who live in Riverview Towers river rats because we live by the dirty river. Maybe there are rats in the river, but I never saw any dirty old rodent in my apartment, no way. You can eat scrambled eggs off the floor in my kitchen, it's so clean. Jazzy's, too.

"Don't mind them," Jazzy says. "They're just jealous 'cause we're happy."

Jazzy and I line our drippy boots along the wall, side by side. We start humming that new Candy song again right at the same time and burst out giggling. "Mr. Otis is coming," Jazzy says. We cover our mouths, but our eyes keep laughing all the same.

The homeroom bell rings. I fish out the notebooks and folders I need for the morning from my locker, plus the poem I wrote that I want to show Mrs. Lullaby, and we hurry to our classroom. I wonder what Mrs. Lullaby's got simmering up sweet for us this morning, maybe some plans for Valentine's Day. I smile at the sign on our door: *Mrs. Lullaby's Smarties.*

❀ ❀ ❀

A lady who is not Mrs. Lullaby is sitting at Mrs. Lullaby's desk.

"Who are you?" I blurt out.

The lady's nose hardens like a clothespin on the laundry line.

"Miss Fagin," she says. "Your substitute teacher."

Fakin? Did she say "faking"? Yes, please, let this be a joke.

The lady points to the blackboard.

MISS FAGIN

"Where's Mrs. Lullaby?" I ask.

"On leave," Miss Fagin says.

My heart sinks into my stomach. "Why? Where is she? Is Mrs. Lullaby okay?"

"Mrs. Lullaby left us?" Jazzy says, her voice cracking like she's going to cry. Some classmates gather around.

"No," I say, loudly, like my words will make it not so. "Mrs. Lullaby would never leave us."

I think of Mrs. Lullaby's silver suitcase, with the stickers from all the amusement parks she's been to where she rides those Wildcat roller coasters she loves, and how she collects our worries every day in that suitcase and then tosses those worries out the window to ease our minds so we can learn better, and how she looks at me like I'm *real*, like she's so happy to see me, ME, Sunny Holiday, every day, and how she makes school more fun than summer, and how she loves us, really loves us. . . .

Other kids start asking about Mrs. Lullaby, too.

Clap-clap-clap-clap-clap!! — Miss Fagin's hands slap the whole room quiet. "Time's wasting," she says, pointing to the clock. "Take your seats, ladies and gentlemen. I'm sure Mr. Otis will send a letter home explaining everything to your parents."

Mr. Otis. No surprise. I bet he's to blame. He doesn't like Mrs. Lullaby's ways. All Mr. Otis talks about are rules. All he cares about are tests.

All Mrs. Lullaby talks about is us. All she cares about is teaching.

The one and only time that no-smile principal ever visited our classroom, he walked about reading our original poems hanging like little sheets on the laundry lines Mrs. Lullaby strung from wall to wall. I sat there all excited, waiting, just waiting for him to burst out nearly singing with praise about our clever ideas and beautiful images and paint-a-picture words and rhythms.

Mr. Otis cleared his throat and said, "Very nice, class," and then, "I do hope we're emphasizing correct spelling and grammar here, Mrs. Lullaby."

I felt stung by a bee. Mrs. Lullaby's face turned red. I couldn't look at Jazzy.

Please come back, Mrs. Lullaby.

I slink like a wet old towel into my chair and stare out the window.

Gray clouds, gray sky, gray heart.

Where are you, Mrs. Lullaby?

Please don't leave us.

Please don't leave me.

Please.

CHAPTER FOUR

Street Shells

Soon there will be dandelions.

I study the gray cement sidewalk like a book as Jazzy and I walk home from school. It's colder than the freezer cases at Save-a-Lot grocery store out here. The lacy white ballerina snowflakes from the last storm have melted away, and now the streets are showing off their ugly garbage again.

Mrs. Lullaby read us a book once about a girl who goes on vacation with her family to the ocean every summer, every single summer. She is so lucky. I sure would love to see the ocean someday. In the story, the girl walks on a long sandy beach with a plastic pail collecting her "sea treasures," as she calls them — dainty yellow shells, striped purple ones, big orange and pink swirly shells you can hear the waves swooshin' in, black rocks with diamond sparkles, wave-smoothed sea glass, brown and green, but mostly shells, lots and lots of shells.

If I had a pail right now this minute, I could collect treasures, too, *street shells* I could call them, except there's nothing very pretty about street shells — nasty orange burger wrappers, broken brown bottles, gold and silver lottery stubs, and slimy globs of gum, lots and lots of gum, red, pink, white, green.

When we turn the corner, sunlight hits my face. I look down and squint my eyelashes together. For a second, the street shells shimmer like jewels — red rubies, white diamonds, green emeralds, silver and gold.

"Sunny?" Jazzy says.

I open my eyes wide and the street is sad real again.

But soon there will be dandelions.

Proud, strong, happy yellow dandelions.

The most beautiful flowers in the world.

In just a few months, May, maybe even April, those sunny smiley faces will be popping up all over — in the scrubby squares of grass, the trashy empty lots, straight up through cracks in the pavement, even. Those baby bright suns will shine all summer long, the fall, too, straight up until the winter frost.

I saw a skinny dandelion in a shiny coat of ice the day before Christmas last year. That was a nice present. Free, too.

My daddy, whose one job used to be mowing lawns, said that *some* people try to poison dandelions dead if they spot them on their property. Can you imagine that? Who would want to kill a flower? *Cold.* That's all that is. Some people are just born with mean genes.

"Bloom like a dandelion, baby girl." That's what my daddy always says. "A dandelion is a powerful flower. There's a 'lion' right in its name."

What's so dandy about a dandelion?

A dandelion's little but it ROARS!

My lips scrunch up and my nose starts to drip and my glasses get cloudy from the tears when I think of my daddy so far away. He's in prison, Mount Burden Correctional Facility, three long hours from here. Daddy made a big mistake, and he's very sorry for it, and if he keeps up his good behavior he might get parole and come home this summer.

Summer seems my whole life away.

I miss my daddy so much. Momma and I haven't seen him since before Halloween. In November, Mount Burden had an "internal problem" and said nobody could visit. In December, Momma got called in to work at the last minute by her boss, Mr. Feeney, such a meanie grump. Then last month, Momma and I got in a snow accident in our friend Mrs. Gordon's ship — it's not really a ship, just a huge old Cadillac car she lets us borrow sometimes — and by the time Momma and I got towed out of the snow, Visiting Day was over.

But then I was on TV, all five channels, when the mayor came to Riverview Towers, and Daddy saw me! He saw me telling Mayor Little what I thought he should be doing for the people of Riverton, especially the kids, and how we should have a holiday and, well, a very nice prison guard let Daddy call me quick to say how proud he was of his baby girl.

"I'm sorry, Sunny," Daddy said, crying into the phone. "I promise I'll never let you and your momma down again."

I told Daddy the only promise I wanted was that we'd always stay together as a family. I told Daddy that when he gets out on parole, he should start drawing again. My daddy is mad talented. You should see the pictures in his portfolio under his and Momma's bed!

That's the wrong place for that portfolio, if you ask me. I think that's the reason why things went so dark for my daddy. His art is his light and he hid it under his bed.

I think everybody's born with a special light inside — like a birthday-candle-size flicker in your heart — and if you don't shine it and share it and let it glow — eventually it grows smaller and smaller and smaller until *poof,* it's gone. Then all you've got is dark and cold inside.

Daddy thinks he can't make a living pencil-sketching people's faces. I know he's wrong because my daddy draws so close to real you'd think it was a photo from a camera.

I told Daddy that I'd ask Mayor Little to help him get a good-paying job when he gets out on parole. He can do his art on weekends, in his free time. *Free time.*

I can't wait for my daddy to be free. I can't wait for time with him.

February Visiting Day is this Sunday. Whoopee!! I'm going to start making Daddy some Valentines tonight. Not just one card for the four-teenth, but a whole month's worth, one heart a day with a happy message on each to keep the sad away until Momma and I can see him again in March.

"Sunny. *Sunny.*" Jazzy is yanking my arm. "Where are you, girl? Don't you hear me talking to you?"

"Sorry, Jazzy. What were you saying?" I don't tell Jazzy I was thinking about my daddy. At least I know where my daddy is and that he loves me. Jazzy hasn't heard from her father in years. She and her mother, Jo-Jo, don't know where he is or if he's still alive, even. That's just wrong. If I ever see Jazzy's father again, I'm going to tell him so. Yes, I am.

"I said Valentine's Day is coming," Jazzy says. "We decided that holiday was good enough, right?"

Last month, Jazzy and I were making decorations for Girls' Night, the dance parties we help our mommas put on for the ladies and girls in our building. I was saying how sad it is for the poor old month of January to be stuck right in between all the fun of Santa in December and candy in February, and the next thing you know we were going through the calendar and rating all the months, figuring out which ones already had good holidays and which months needed some improvement.

We decided six months — February, April, July, October, November, and December — already had fun-enough holidays, but the other six needed help. Those sorry six — January, March, May, June, August, and September — they all needed some kind of new holiday every kid could look forward to. I said January should get the most important holiday — Kid's Day — and that maybe we could also cook up something fun for the other ones, too.

We're planning to have the first annual Kid's Day next year — just eleven months away!! Mayor Little wants a preliminary report when we have lunch this Saturday. Ooh . . . that reminds me. I need to organize my committee to start planning. We'll need lots and lots of good ideas.

"Right, Sunny?" Jazzy says again, sighing loudly, exasperated with me. "February's good with Valentine's, right?"

We're in front of Daisy's Lucky Buck, the everything-for-a-dollar store we love to shop at. The window is all decorated in pink and red Valentine's stuff, teddy bears and lovey-dove cards and boxes of heart-shaped chocolates. I think about Daddy. I think about Mrs. Lullaby. For some reason I think of the red-hooded brother at the bus stop. I get a sparkler idea — *spark, spark, spark* — in my head.

"Yeah, Jazzy. Valentine's is fine all right, but maybe we can make it even sweeter. Come on. Let's go in. I've got some leftover Christmas money to spend."

After we finish shopping, we stop at Mrs. Milo's store for cupcakes, two in a pack. We lick the frosting first and then pop the cakes whole into our mouths so that our cheeks bulge out like baby hippos. We giggle. I nearly choke. Something shiny on the street catches my eye. I bend down to look.

Somebody's old, broken, silver Christmas tree ornament.

I pick up the biggest piece. It's like a mirror. I smile at myself in there.

I pick up the other pieces, put my "street shells" in my pocket, and link Jazzy's arm to head home.

CHAPTER FIVE

A Bump in the Road

*Momma says you need a plan
if you have a dream.*

Riverview Towers apartment building is six stories high, with all the same windows, all the same doors, all the same ceilings, all the same floors. Living here could make a person feel awfully "same" if you didn't know for certain you were special.

I fish out our little mailbox key.

Empty, not even a bill. *Come on, Daddy. Why don't you write to me?*

"Mrs. Depaki's making curry again," Jazzy says.

Mmm. I take a deep sniff in and smile. *Yumm.*

Walking into our lobby right about now each day — when at-home folks are starting to make dinner and at-work folks' Crock-Pot stews that have been simmering all day are bubbling up ready to serve — it's like our own mini version of the International Food Festival they have across the river every summer. Curry and basil, onions and garlic, fish frying, chili simmering, so many different, delicious aromas.

You might walk by and see the outside of Riverview Towers, all the same windows, all the same doors, and think we're all the same, too, but come inside about five o'clock P.M. and you'll have to eat your words. Eat your words.

"Pun intended," as Mrs. Lullaby taught us. Pun intended. Fun intended, too.

Momma and I live on the third floor, 3-B. Jazzy and her mother, Jo-Jo Fine, and Jazzy's grandmother, Sister Queen, live upstairs in 4-C. Our balconies are so close, I can blow Jazzy a bubble, she can toss me a ball, so near we don't need a phone. Good thing, because phone minutes cost money. Eyes-to-eyes talk doesn't cost a penny. Another sparkler idea goes off in my head. I'm going to add *eyes-to-eyes talk* to the list of free things Momma and I are making a book about.

Our book is called *Free All Year*. Right now we're writing it with wash-off colored markers on our living room wall, but when it's finished, we're going to get it printed up and published and go on the Oprah show and our book will sell so many copies we'll be able to buy a house on Hill Street.

That's the plan. Momma says you need a plan if you have a dream.

Jazzy and I get on the elevator. It smells like old-people medicine. Jazzy presses #3 for me and #4 for her. Just as the doors are closing, Eli Stokes pushes his arm in. "Wait up," he says, all huffing out of breath, carrying a basketball. Eli's nice. He's in our class. Jazzy has a crush on him. I think he crushes her, too.

"Hey, Jazzy," Eli says. "Hey, Sunny."

Eli hits #5 and stares at Jazzy. Jazzy stares at the elevator numbers lighting up, #1 . . . *beep* . . . #2 . . . *beep* . . . Jazzy is studying those numbers like a mathematics test question, or like maybe somehow those numbers got mixed up today and she better pay attention or she'll miss her floor.

I giggle quiet inside my head. *Jazzy and Eli, sitting in a tree . . .*

When the doors part open on my floor, I secret-elbow Jazzy gently as I go. She purses her lips so she won't giggle.

I'm supposed to go straight to Mrs. Sherman's place, *yuck*, but first I want to get some Valentine-making stuff from my house in case I have time after homework to start my cards for Daddy. Mrs. Sherman runs an after-school program. Some days — unless I have permission to go to Jazzy's — I go there until Momma gets home from work.

Momma is studying to be a nurse or maybe a doctor, but right now she's a "suite-keeper," a fancy name for room cleaner, at the big Crowne Plaza Hotel across the river in Springtown. With Daddy doing time and money so tight, Momma has to work double-hard for our family.

Outside my door, I stick the first key in, then the second, and — *surprise!!* — Momma is home early! She's sitting at the table with the bill box and her checkbook.

"Momma, what are you doing home already?"

I hear a leap-landing off my bed and then my cat, Queen Jade, comes to greet me, *welcome home.* "Hey, Jadie." I pick her up, scratch the white patch on her black fur head, and snuggle her in close. "Hi, baby. I missed you." I kiss her head. She nose-kisses me. The tips of her ears are cold.

Momma slips her bill-paying worry look into an envelope along with a check and seals them both up good. "Get over here, girl," she says.

I put Jade down and go to Momma. She hugs me tight. "Your nose is froze," she says with a laugh, cupping her warm hand over my nose like a mitten.

"My toes are, too, that's how it goes." I love to rhyme, using words like music. Maybe someday I'll write lyrics like Candy Wrapper.

That's if I don't become president like Momma predicts.

The Oprah show is on the TV. Momma and Jazzy's mother, Jo-Jo, *love* Oprah. Momma and Jo-Jo are best friends just like me and Jazzy. They are usually both working when Oprah is on, so they tape the programs and do an "Oprah Marathon" on Sundays at our brunch-fest after First Baptist.

I think Ms. Oprah ought to change her name to *Hope-rah* because that's what that lady does. She gives people hope.

I take off my boots, hang up my coat, and go to my room to change out of my school clothes. *Brrr.* It's cold in here. I put on a turtleneck, sweatpants, and the warm pink fleece sweatshirt Momma gave me for Christmas.

The doorbell buzzes. Maybe it's Jazzy and we can play.

Momma opens the door.

It's Jo-Jo, looking all concerned.

"Sherry, girl," Jo-Jo says to my mother. "I came as fast as I could."

My mother puts her finger to her lips, *shhh*, and turns back to see if I heard.

"Momma, what's wrong? Are you all right?"

"I'm fine, Sunny," she says. "Just a little work issue, nothing important. Now please go do your homework while I talk to Jo-Jo for a bit."

"Yes, Momma." I go to my room. *What work issue?* I hear the coffeepot gurgling and Momma and Jo-Jo talking in low voices in the kitchen. I take out my assignment notebook. I do division first. Mrs. Lullaby says I'm a regular "math whiz." They're still talking out there. I study for my science quiz. They're *still* talking out there. I copy out twenty vocabulary words, remembering how I knew nearly all the words on that big state test last month. I can't wait to find out how I did! Finally, history. I answer the three questions in complete sentences, and then I'm done.

Maybe I'll write a poem about street shells. I remember the cool poem about icicles I brought in to show Mrs. Lullaby this morning. My heart squeezes.

Where are you, Mrs. Lullaby? I hope you are all right.

It sure is cold as Alaska in here. I put on a second sweatshirt and zip it, pulling up the hood to warm my head. I picture the sad-eyes boy all slumped over in the bus house this morning. Why was he so down? I push the hood off.

Finally, I hear Momma and Jo-Jo say good-bye.

In the kitchen, Momma's back is to me and her body is shaking. She's got her arms wrapped around her like she's giving herself a hug.

"Momma?"

She jumps. She quick wipes the tears from her face, but I see them.

"Momma, what? Tell me, please. Is it Daddy? Is Daddy okay?"

"Yes, honey, far as I know. In fact, there's a letter for you on the counter."

I rush to the counter, then stop. "Wait. First tell me what's wrong with *you*."

"I got a pink slip today."

"What's that mean?"

"The holidays are over and business is down at the Crowne, way, way down. They can't give those expensive rooms away, the economy has gotten so bad. Mr. Feeney doesn't need as many cleaners. The most recent hires had to go first, fair is fair."

My heart is pounding. "You lost your job, Momma?"

"I'm sure I'll find another," she says. "Or

maybe they'll hire me back when business picks up again."

"What about school?" I say. My momma's been working for her college degree — one course a semester, that's all we can afford — for as long as I can remember.

"This class is paid for," she says, "but I may need to skip next semester."

"No," I say. "We'll figure something out."

"Sunny, please," Momma says. "I don't want you worrying about these things. This is just a bump in the road. I'm the parent. I'll handle this."

"We are a family," I say. "We handle things together."

"Oh, Sunny." Momma lets out a sob, then looks ashamed, like she shouldn't be crying. I feel so bad that Momma's hurting, I start to cry, too.

I go to Momma and hug her. Neither of us says it, but we are both thinking it.

Daddy ought to be here. He ought to be here taking care of us.

Momma pulls away from me and dries her face. She blows her nose and then tosses the tissue into the trash. "Come on, Sunny," she says, trying to smile herself into a happier mood. "Go get your coat. We're going to Taco-Bama's."

"No," I say.

"What?" Momma looks surprised. "You love burritos."

"No."

"How about Chico's for some barbecue, then?"

I shake my head, no. "We've got to save our money."

"But . . ." Momma starts to protest, then she stops and stares into my eyes. My momma is a good talker but she's an even better listener. Momma knows when to stop and listen, really listen. It's one of her best talents.

Momma walks to the desk, opens the box of markers and takes out a purple, her favorite color. Momma stands there considering our beautiful wall book, *Free All Year*, featuring all of the wonderful things we love that are free. We plan to think up 365 free things, one for each day of the year. So far we've got two hundred. All the words are in different colors and written on arcs like the bands of a rainbow.

Momma finds a spot and prints *common sense*.

"Common sense saves cents," I say.

"What's that called again, my smart daughter?" Momma says. "When two words sound alike but have different meanings and spell —"

"Homonyms," I say.

Momma laughs. "That's my smart sweet Sunny girl."

CHAPTER SIX

My Gratitudes

No sense dwelling on the past.

Momma defrosts the container of ziti and meat-balls that our grumpy building superintendent, the "Soup," Mr. Petrofino, gave us as a sort-of Christmas present.

When we were little, Jazzy and I used to joke about what kind of soup Mr. Petrofino was ... Chicken noodle? Tomato? Alphabet?

I don't think Mr. Petrofino originally planned

a Christmas present for me and Momma, but after we brought him a plate of sugar cookies, two days later he rang our bell. Mr. Petrofino looked nervous standing there in his suit and tie with that little folded handkerchief he always has in his top pocket. "Happy Holidays," he said, and he handed me a plastic container of lasagna with *Petrofino* printed across the top.

I nearly squeezed his face in the door trying to keep it closed enough so he wouldn't catch sight of our word wall. I'm pretty sure that writing a wall book is against Riverview Towers building regulations, even if the words are in washable markers that we're going to clean off and paint over fresh when we move to our new house on Hill Street someday soon.

Mr. Petrofino probably thought I was really rude not to invite him in.

"No need to return the dish," he said.

Momma and I enjoyed that lasagna very much, and when I returned the Soup's container filled with Momma's famous banana muffins as a thank-you, that old grumpy-grump man almost cracked a smile. He had music playing that day, opera, I think it was. There was a portrait of a family on the wall over his sofa, blown up so big the people nearly looked life-size. A lady and a man and a girl. The man looked like a young Mr. Petrofino. The lady was pretty. The girl looked my age. "Is that your family?" I said.

Mr. Petrofino looked up at the picture. "Once," he said.

Oh, I felt so sad for him. I wanted to ask him where his wife was, and his daughter, what's her name and how old was she, but I could tell Mr. Petrofino didn't want me to pry. And Momma had already warned me that he was a very private person. "Don't be all getting up in his business," she said. "Just give him the muffins and say thanks again for the dinner."

Well, the week after that, Mr. Petrofino rang our doorbell again. I moved out into the hallway and closed the door behind me so he wouldn't see our wall book. "Don't want to let the cat out," I said.

"I made too much ziti and meatballs," he said, holding the container out to me. "Maybe you and your mother can use it. And keep the dish. I don't need it."

Momma makes us a salad. "How many f-and-g's did you have today?" she says.

One of Momma's resolutions for the new year is to be sure we eat nine servings of f-and-g's, fruits and vegetables, every day. "Nine's fine" is the rhyme we made to remember.

Let's see . . . I had orange juice and a banana at breakfast, green beans and corn and fruit salad at lunch, an apple at snack time. . . . "Six," I tell her.

"Good girl," Momma says, setting some broccoli on the stove to steam.

I light the dinner candles, one on either side of the red poinsettia plant our neighbor Mrs. Gordon gave us last month. Momma and I always like to have candles and flowers, real flowers, no plastic stuff for us, on our dinner table.

Momma pours our milk. We bow our heads, say grace, and dig in.

"Wow, is Mr. Petrofino a good cook," I say.

"These meatballs are even better than his lasagna. I can't wait to tell him so."

"I'm sure he'll appreciate that," Momma says, spearing a cucumber with her fork.

"Are we going to fill his container back up with something again this time?" I ask.

"What do you think?" Momma says.

"Yes."

"Then yes it is," Momma says, smiling. "Maybe some cupcakes for Valentine's."

After we do the dishes, Momma reads me the letter from Mr. Otis that came in the mail today. It seems that Mrs. Lullaby has been put on "disciplinary leave" for "misleading her fourth-grade class about their performance on a certain practice test leading up to the NYS-mandated achievement tests administered last month . . ."

"What?!" I shout. "Is that man saying Mrs. Lullaby lied? Mrs. Lullaby would never lie to us. He's just trying to find a way to get rid of her because he doesn't like the way she teaches. She'd rather read another book to us than write some stupid report for him. We are the smartest fourth grade in the state. Yes, we are. Just wait until those scores come back. Just wait until that stupid man . . ."

"Sunny."

"That mean old never-smile . . ."

"Sunny!"

"That *principal* . . ."

"That's better."

"Just wait until I give him a piece of my mind."

"Be respectful, Sunny."

"Yes, Momma. I will. Mrs. Lullaby won't tolerate anything less."

Momma comes in to say good night.

I'm wearing my warmest pajamas and my bathrobe, and Momma puts an extra quilt over the one Grand-Gran made me. Momma wants to try putting that thermostat down to fifty-five degrees at night to save money.

"Once upon a time, there was a boy in a red hood sitting in a bus house. . . ."

That's how I start tonight's three-thing story.

The three-thing story is a tradition Daddy started when I was little. He would make up a story using three things we saw that day.

Now I'm the storyteller in our family. Momma prefers to listen.

When Momma leaves, I slide my night-light close to my head and read my letter from Daddy over and over. He loved the last batch of pictures I made him, "especially the ones with the poems on them" and "the dandelions on every page." He says, "I love you, baby girl. Can't wait to see you."

Daddy sent me some artwork, too. *X-Pac*, *Willie*, and *Jerome*. I smile at the faces Daddy sketched on a white handkerchief with colored pencils. Daddy bought the pencils at the prison commissary with money some inmates gave him for drawing portraits of them to send back home. *X-Pac* and *Willie* and *Jerome*. I'm glad my daddy has some friends in that cold old place. Prison must feel so lonely.

I snuggle down under my quilts with the letter and Valentine, the teddy bear Daddy gave me last Valentine's Day. Just before Daddy made that really big mistake and ruined everything. . . . No sense dwelling on the past. I stop thinking sad things.

"Here's to the future," I say, looking into Valentine's big brown eyes.

Valentine is listening very intently. He is such a smart bear.

"There has to be a way to help Momma get her job back and Mrs. Lullaby get our class back." I yawn, tired from a long, long day. "Then it would be an extra-sweet Valentine's Day for sure."

I read a chapter from my book for school. I'm three chapters ahead of where we're supposed to be, but that's okay because I like reading them over again. Each time I do, I discover something new. Good books have layers like that, Mrs. Lullaby says.

When I'm finished reading, I say my gratitudes. Momma taught me to pray like this, counting off ten things with my fingers that I'm grateful for each day. On especially good days, toes can be added.

I open my palms toward my face.

"Dear God . . . thank you for . . ." I start counting with my left thumb. "Momma, Daddy, Jazzy, Mrs. Lullaby, and Valentine." I kiss my bear's furry head.

"Meow!" Queen Jade jumps up on the bed all jealous. I laugh and scratch all around her ears and she nestles in beside me. "Good girl."

I continue praying with my right-hand pinkie. "And thank you for Queen Jade, and Ms. Candy Wrapper, wherever in the world she's singing tonight, and street shells . . . I like that, *street shells*, God, do you? I wonder, God, did I make that name up original? Maybe you could let me know."

Two more fingers . . . "And thank you for the wall book Momma and I are making, and . . ." I yawn . . . one more . . . "Mr. Petrofino's Italian cooking, especially the meatballs."

Just before I drift off to sleep, I picture the sad-slumped brother in the graffiti-covered bus house this morning, and I send him a happy wish.

CHAPTER SEVEN

Conversation Hearts

What if the words really mattered?

"My momma wants to have a little surprise birthday party dinner for your momma tonight," Jazzy says next morning on the way to school.

"But her birthday isn't until Monday," I say.

"I know," Jazzy says, "but Momma and Sister Queen thought maybe Sherry could use a little extra-early cake and presents this year."

Jazzy doesn't talk about my momma losing her job.

"Come round at six o'clock tonight, okay?" Jazzy says.

"We'll be there," I say. "Thanks."

"So," Jazzy says, "have you thought about how you're going to improve Valentine's Day?"

Who has time for holidays? I need to help Momma find a job and I need to talk some sense into Mr. Otis so he brings Mrs. Lullaby right straight back to our class, do not pass go, do not collect two hundred dollars.

"You said you wanted to make Valentine's sweeter, Sunny. How?"

"I don't know," I say, kicking a frozen sneaker out of our path on the sidewalk. What's a sneaker doing on a street? Seems like you'd know if you lost one, litterbug.

"Something about candy?" Jazzy suggests.

"Nah. That's all Valentine's is right now. Candy and cards. A heart-shaped thing of chocolates if you're lucky, more likely one of those little boxes of conversation hearts and a shoe box full of cards from everybody in the class — cards that aren't really special because we buy them all the same at Lucky Buck and sign our name all the same, then throw them all out the next day."

"*Conversation hearts?*" Jazzy says. "You mean the little heart candies with words on them like 'Be Mine' and 'True Love'? I didn't know they were called conversation hearts."

"Yep, that's right," I say.

"Why do they call them that?" Jazzy says.

"I don't know. Maybe the person who invented them thought that if you gave one to somebody, it might help you start talking with them — you know, have a conversation."

Jazzy laughs. "That's sweet," she says. "That's nice."

I try to get Mr. Otis's attention walking into school, but no luck. How can I get the chance to talk with him? Mrs. Lullaby would give me permission to go to his office if I said I had a good reason. But this new teacher, Miss Fagin, she'll probably just say no.

"Not without a note from your parents," Miss Fagin says.

I knew it. "But, please, Miss Fagin. It's important. I've got to talk with —"

"Mr. Otis is a very busy man," Miss Fagin says. "Now please take your seat."

During math, I finish my last problem, close my notebook, and place my hands, palms down, on my desk like Miss Fagin instructed us to do. She has lots of new rules like that. Mrs. Lullaby would have let us take out a "your-choice book" or whatever we wanted as long as we were quiet while we waited for our classmates to finish.

I look out the window.

A red bird flits onto a branch, then away. A snowflake, then another, and another, and another, dance down freely from the sky. The red bird flits back. It stands out like a heart against the black tree and white clouds.

I think about conversation hearts. The little words stamp-printed on them. Fun, but all the same, no one really pays attention. . . .

What if the words really mattered?

That thought sparks in my head like a firefly and warms me up. *What if the words really mattered?* I reach down and grab out my writer's notebook, pick up my pen, and start writing fast as I can so I won't miss a thing I'm hearing inside.

Conversation hearts. What if the words really mattered? What if you really thought about the person you were giving a heart to and you wrote something that . . .

"Sunny Holiday," Miss Fagin says.

I hear her calling me, but I keep writing.

I'm not dissing her. It's just that Mrs. Lullaby taught us that you never know when a good idea — a sparkler idea — is going to come, and when one does you've got to catch it fast as you can. Good ideas burn bright as sparklers on the Fourth of July, then before you know it, *poof*, they're gone. Good ideas glow, teasing you — *glow, glow, glow* — and you better catch them quick on paper like fireflies in a mayonnaise jar, or they'll fly off into somebody else's mind-yard, *good-bye*.

"Miss Holiday?" Miss Fagin calls me again, louder this time.

"Sunny," Jazzy whispers across the aisle, worried for me.

I look quick around. Everybody's got their palms down. Manny Woodson, he's cute, smiles at me. I hurry and finish my last sentence.

There, done. I put my pen down and close my notebook, my body all shaking, excited from the writing.

"Sunny Holiday!" Miss Fagin says sharply, really steaming now.

"Yes, Miss Fagin? I'm sorry."

"I'd like to speak with you up here, please."

"You're in trouble," Davina Bishop whispers gleefully.

"Did you finish your math?" Miss Fagin asks me when I reach her desk.

"Yes, ma'am, a long time ago."

"Then why weren't your hands on your desk as I instructed?"

"Because I needed my hands to write."

My friend Kathina in the front row giggles.

That did come out a bit rude.

"I'm sorry," I say. "I'm not trying to be disrespectful. It's just . . ." I lower my voice so only Miss Fagin can hear. "It's just I had a really good idea and I wanted to write it down so I wouldn't forget."

"An idea about mathematics?" Miss Fagin says.

"No," I say. "An idea about love."

Miss Fagin's clothespin nose hardens but there's a soft wave of something across her mouth. I can't tell if it's a happy wave or sad or mad or what.

"This is math time," Miss Fagin says quietly. "We do writing fifth period."

I listen respectfully, but I don't say anything.

Miss Fagin studies my face.

I can tell this lady doesn't like me.

"All right, then," she says, raising her voice. "Just don't let it happen again."

Can't promise that, I think to myself as I walk back to my seat. The way I get such good ideas? I can't promise I won't grab my notebook and pen the next time a firefly floats in my head. No, ma'am. I'm sorry, but I can't promise that at all.

Davina smiles nasty and crosses her arms all satisfied, like *ha-ha, you got yours*, as I walk back to my desk.

I never ever got in trouble with Mrs. Lullaby. She loves my writing. She hangs up the best pieces we write, mostly poems, on the laundry lines around our classroom. I have the most poem-laundry of anybody. I'm not bragging. It's a fact. Mr. Otis wants her to take down the laundry and put up lists of grammar words, I know. I heard him telling her. Crazy principal. That man needs some enlightenment.

I stick my tongue out at Davina.

"River rat," she says.

At the end of the day, Miss Fagin asks for a volunteer to go pick up a package she left in the teachers' lounge. Jazzy's hand springs up.

"Pick a partner to accompany you," Miss Fagin says.

I'm out of my seat before I even hear Jazzy say my name.

The door to the teachers' lounge is open. Mrs. Lullaby's best teacher friend, Mrs. Weaver, is talking with one of the third-grade teachers, Ms. Thomas. Their backs are to us.

"Otis has had it in for Lu since he got here," Mrs. Weaver says.

"Lu" is short for "Lucretia," Mrs. Lullaby's first name.

"First she refused to fail any of her kids. She said, 'I'll work with them myself personally all summer if I have to. Children shouldn't be stamped a failure because grown-ups didn't do right by them.'"

I put my finger to my lips to tell Jazzy to be quiet. I want to hear what they're saying about Mrs. Lullaby.

"Then Lu refused to fill out any more blasted state reports," Mrs. Weaver says. "'I'm a teacher, not a calculator,' she told Otis. 'Let me do the job I was hired for.'"

Ms. Thomas nods her head. "And let me tell you, Lu didn't mince words on her evaluation of Mr. Otis last May. I told her to be careful, but she said, 'What do I have to lose? I'm nearly to retirement. Only ones losing here are the kids.'"

The final bell rings. "Excuse us," Jazzy says. The teachers look up and smile. "We're here to get a package for Miss Fagin."

There's a bulletin board on the wall. I scan it quickly, hoping maybe there's a posting about a job at New Hope. It would be so nice to have Momma here with me. There are fliers about a staff meeting, a walking club, a diet program, a candle party, and one-two-three-four postings about Girl Scout cookies. Nothing about a job.

CHAPTER EIGHT

A Playdate for the Queens

❀ ❀ ❀

They take good care of each other like that.

When Jazzy and I get home from school, Miss Fontenot, the dance lady who lives in 2-G, is getting out of a taxi with her grocery bags from Save-a-Lot. The taxi driver is helping her load the bags into a fold-up cart on wheels.

Miss Fontenot used to be a famous dancer, starred in shows and all, and after that she ran a dance school. There was a waiting list to get in, it was so popular. But that was a long time ago. Now she keeps to herself and doesn't talk much to anyone. Sometimes she moves like she's sleepwalking, not quite sure where she's going, mumbling to herself. But every once in a while, Miss Fontenot gets a burst of energy and does something fruit-loopy. Like last Fourth of July barbecue, we were all on the street in our bathing suits getting down with the DJ from JAMS 96.3, and Miss Fontenot sashayed out in a leotard, tutu, and tights and started leaping about like Tinker Bell from *Peter Pan*.

Miss Fontenot is crazy but she's nice. She let me and Jazzy borrow hula skirts for our Hawaii Girls' Night last month. We always invite her to our dance parties, but Miss Fontenot hardly ever comes. Too bad, because pretty much all we do is dance. She'd enjoy herself.

"Are you going to invite Manny Woodson to Girls' Night?" Jazzy asks.

"No way," I say. Manny is in our class. Yes, he's cute, but no, I don't like him.

Girls' Night is a week from Saturday, on Valentine's. Jo-Jo and Jazzy are hosting. Jo-Jo said maybe we should invite some boys and men this time. It's not that we don't like boys, it's just that when the parties started it was only us four, me and Momma and Jazzy and Jo-Jo, and then it grew little by little with more ladies and girls from our building. I'm not sure how I feel about having boys and men there. What if they make fun of us?

"I think Momma's inviting Chief Slade to come," Jazzy says.

Chief Slade is a firefighter who lives up on the sixth floor. Everybody knows the Chief and Jo-Jo like each other. Jazzy and I have a bet going on when they'll have their first date. Jazzy bet February. I bet March.

"He is one fine man," I heard Momma telling Jo-Jo. "If he's too shy to ask you out, then step up and ask him, sista. You've been in mourning long enough. You deserve some happiness, girl."

I think about poor Momma on Valentine's Day. All alone without Daddy, nobody to dance with at the party. I won't have anybody to dance with, either, because I'm not inviting Manny Woodson, no matter what Jazzy says. No way.

"Hello, Miss Fontenot," I say, holding the elevator door until she wheels her grocery cart in. There's a bouquet of purple tulips in plastic and a long skinny loaf of bread, French I think, sprouting out of the top bag. I see she's got a hunk of cheese, *Gruyère* it says on the label, and a bag of grapes.

Miss Fontenot's blue eyes meet my brown ones. She seems deep down in the dumps today, not a spark of happy in there at all.

I feel bad for the dance lady. I smile to try and cheer her up, but she looks away.

"Are you okay, Miss Fontenot?" Jazzy asks. She's holding the door for Mr. Williams, Sister Queen's friend, who's making his way toward us with his cane. He tips his hat and nods at us. "Thank you kindly, Jazzy. Afternoon, lovely ladies."

Miss Fontenot makes a sad sound and scrunches her scarf up around her mouth.

"Can we do something to help, Miss Fontenot?" I say. She doesn't answer.

On the second floor, as the elevator door is closing, Miss Fontenot mumbles something, not to us . . . to herself, real quiet.

I'm not sure, but I think Miss Fontenot said, "Take me to Paris."

I'm so worried about Momma losing her job, but it sure is nice having her home!

There's a plate of home-baked oatmeal raisin cookies on the counter, and Momma is cutting out Jell-O jigglers, strawberry, in the shape of hearts.

"Jigglers," Jazzy shouts. "My favorite. All right!"

When Jazzy goes into the bathroom to wash her hands, I tell Momma all casual that we're invited to Jazzy and Jo-Jo's for dinner. I don't mention it's a surprise for her birthday.

"Okay, sure," Momma says, trying to sound happy, but I can hear the job-worry in her voice.

"I checked the bulletin board in the teachers' lounge for job postings," I say.

Momma smiles. "That was nice of you, honey. But I don't have a teaching degree," she says. "I'm training for the medical field."

"I know," I say, "but maybe there's something you could do at New Hope."

"They've already got a janitor," Momma says. She fills the sink with water and squeezes in soap to scrub off the cookie pans.

I watch a few bubbles float up toward Momma's face. My momma is so smart and strong and beautiful. My momma is regal. She deserves a crown and a golden robe. Then I picture her cleaning nasty old disgusting toilet bowls at that fancy hotel she got fired from and it makes me want to spit. Sherry Holiday deserves better than toilet bowls. She deserves to finish her degree. She deserves a job that's worthy of her talents.

After we finish our snack, Jazzy goes upstairs to bring down her cat, Queen Penny, so that Penny and Queen Jade can have a playdate.

We adopted our cats together from the animal shelter for Christmas. They are "tuxedo cats," all black with white paws and white patches under their chins and on the tips of their ears. They look like twins, except Jazzy's cat, Queen Penny, has copper-colored eyes, and my cat, Queen Jade, has jade green. Those cats are best friends just like me and Jazzy.

The queens are so happy to see each other! At first they meow and stare and then Jadie paw-swipes Penny and takes off running. Penny chases after her and the next thing you know they're meowing and play-biting and tussling all friendly, having a ball.

After Jazzy and I finish our homework, we get out the cat brushes and brush the queens really well. We don't want them choking on hair balls. When we're finished, we reward them with three heart-shaped cat treats each.

Jazzy reads the ingredients on the treat package. *"Uggh . . ."* she says. "Listen to what's in these things. Hydrolyzed chicken liver . . ."

"Nasty," I say. "Doesn't sound like a treat to me."

"Wait, it gets nastier," Jazzy says. "Fish oil . . ."

"Yuck!"

Queen Penny tries to swipe the package out of Jazzy's hands.

"Sorry, Penny," Jazzy says. "Three treats a day. That's it."

Penny and Jade sniff around our fingers and the floor all hopeful, making their sweet cat eyes at us, hoping we change our minds. Then, when they are finally sure we mommas mean it, they leap up on the couch, in the warmest spot by the heating vent. Queen Jade licks Queen Penny's coat clean. They take good care of each other like that. Penny falls asleep first, then Jade.

When I look again, they're snuggled up in a circle, paws overlapping, heads tilted in, touching like a heart.

Jazzy leaves, and I go to change my clothes for the surprise birthday dinner tonight. The phone rings. I hear Momma say, "I'm a good driver. No, sorry, I don't have one."

"Who was that, Momma?"

"One of the jobs I called about." Momma sighs. "You need a car for it." Momma puts an X through a square in the newspaper.

We head upstairs to the Fines' apartment. Hip-hop music booming loud inside. I push the buzzer. The music stops. The door opens in. It's all dark inside.

"SURPRISE, SHERRY BABY!!!" Jo-Jo shouts. Someone flicks on the lights.

There's a sweet shining sea of smiling faces. All of Momma's friends from the dance parties.

"Happy birthday, girl," Jazzy's grandmother, Sister Queen, says, scooping Momma up in her arms. "You keep getting prettier and younger-looking every year. How old are you now, *sixteen*?"

Momma laughs. She turns to hug Jo-Jo. "Thank you, girl. You didn't have to. . . ."

"This isn't no *have-to* thing," Jo-Jo says. "It's a *wanna-do*. We all love you, baby."

Dinner is soooooo good. There's fried chicken made Sister Queen's special way, *praise Jesus*, and sweet potato fries and green beans and gravy. Everybody's focusing on my momma, making her the star tonight.

Jo-Jo slices up and serves pieces of the cherry

cheesecake Mrs. Gordon brought. *Yum, yum.* But that was just our appetizer dessert. Sister Queen dims the lights, and Jo-Jo comes out of the kitchen carrying a triple-high chocolate birthday cake, covered with candles.

We all sing.

"Make a good wish, girl," Jo-Jo tells Momma.

Momma looks at me and smiles.

I wink at her. She winks at me. We both know what she's wishing for.

After the cake, Sister Queen hands Momma a straw basket filled with envelopes. Birthday cards. "Open these later, honey," she says.

"Happy birthday, Sherry baby," Jo-Jo says.

"Group hug, group hug," I say. And then everybody gathers around my momma like a blanket, making sure she feels how much she's loved.

Later, back in our apartment, I hear my momma crying in her room. I go to check on her. She's sitting on her bed with all the cards opened around her.

"Oh, Sunny," she says, shaking her head. "Look at this."

There was money in all the cards, but no signatures. Not one person's name, just a *love you, girl* or *hang in there, baby*, a smiley face or a drawn-on heart.

"They knew if they signed their names, I'd make them take their money back. Nobody has extra cash these days. I can't take this. . . ."

"Oh, yes, you can, Momma," I say. "And you know why?"

"Why, baby?"

"Because someday when one of those ladies, your friends, needs a hand, you'll do the same good thing for them."

CHAPTER NINE

Grumps, Slumps, Bumps, and Dumps

Heart-spark. Pass it on.

When I go back to my room, I'm too wide awake to sleep. I take out the Valentine's supplies and stuff I bought at Lucky Buck to make my cards for Daddy.

I draw a heart on each card and write a little happy message inside like *Today's a New Day* and

Keep Up the Good Work and *Dreams Come True with a Plan.*

What if the words really mattered? That firefly comes in my head again. I think about the power just a few itty-bitty little words can have. I think about our president, Barack Obama, who kept on saying "Yes, We Can," until a whole country of people believed we could.

Daddy will love these Valentines. Visiting Day is Sunday, hooray! I can't wait to see my daddy! Momma and I are going to leave early — really, really early this time so there won't be any problems. It's been four whole months since I've seen Daddy. He doesn't know how Momma lost her job yet or what's happened to Mrs. Lullaby.

I can't wait to set that mean old Mr. Otis straight about how Mrs. Lullaby is not a liar. She's the best teacher in the world. Momma wrote me a fine note to give Miss Fagin, saying how I would be meeting with Mayor Little this Saturday and "Sunny would like to include some good news about New Hope from Mr. Otis in her report" and so would she please let me go to his office.

"Now just be sure you get some news so this note is not a lie," Momma said, and I promised I would.

I open up a package of white labels I bought at Lucky Buck. I had a sparkler idea about how to make Valentine's Day sweeter and I want to test something out.

With a fat red marker, I color in one whole label. Then I trace a heart shape, a little bigger than a quarter, in the center with my pencil. I cut out the heart.

A heart-shaped sticker. And a leftover stencil to use to make other stickers.

Maybe a way to make Valentine's Day a little sweeter would be to give a heart sticker to people who need a little extra love. Grumps and slumps. Folks having bumps in the road. Folks down in the dumps. Grumps like Mr. Petrofino and Mr. Otis. Slumps like the red-tent boy in the bus house. Folks having bumps in the road like Momma and Mrs. Lullaby. People down-in-the-dumps depressed like Miss Fontenot.

I make red heart stickers until my eyes get watery. I line the hearts up in a row on the table. They look nice. But something's missing.

Maybe they need some words like the heart cards I made for Daddy.

But I don't know Mr. Petrofino or Mr. Otis well enough to know just what words would make them happier. Or what phrase might make the boy who hides himself in the hood-tent feel encouraged. I wonder what saying might help Momma over her bump in the road or pull Miss

Fontenot out of the dumps? My head's too tired now to think.

Then I remember my street shells.

I take the broken silver ornament pieces out of my coat pocket and lay them on the desk next to the hearts. I break off a small piece of silver ornament and glue it on one of the hearts. I wave it by my desk lamp and the silver catches the light. Just a little flicker, like a firefly. *A love bug.*

That idea makes me laugh. "Punch bug, no punch back," Jazzy and I say when those little round cars go by.

I break off another piece and glue it on the next heart. I try to get it right in the center like on the first heart, but this one sticks a bit farther down. That's okay. It's good that they're different. No two hearts are the same, anyway.

I keep on working, gluing a little spark on

every single heart until they're all finished. Grumps, slumps, bumps, and dumps. What if we stuck stickers on people on Valentine's Day to help them see the light they have inside? A little jumpstart.

Heart-spark. Pass it on.

As I'm falling asleep, I think about conversation hearts. *What if the words really mattered?* I imagine sticking one of these sparkly red stickers I made on Mr. Petrofino's jacket, on Valentine's Day, quick before he can say he doesn't "need it."

Heart-spark, pass it on.

That's all I'll need to say. Mr. Petrofino will hear the words he needs to hear inside his very own heart.

Heart-spark, pass it on.

Heart-spark, pass it on.

Heart-spark, pass it on.

I yawn and say my gratitudes, *good night.*

CHAPTER TEN

Sunny's Bad Mistake

*There's nothing wrong
with my neighborhood.*

In the morning, I post a flier on the bulletin board downstairs in our building lobby, saying any kids who are interested in helping to plan the new Kid's Day holiday are invited to a committee meeting today at four o'clock P.M. in the Community Room. Refreshments provided. Bring your good ideas. I sign it *Sunny Holiday, 3-B.*

I hesitate for a minute because I don't want to seem like I'm bragging, but the truth is the truth and it does sound more important and official, so I add my title underneath my name: *Junior Deputy Mayor, Riverton, New York.*

When Jazzy and I get to school, I tape up another flier. I don't put "3-B" on this one. I sign it *Sunny Holiday, Mrs. Lullaby's Class.*

Miss Fagin reads the note from Momma and says I can go to the principal's office but to "hurry right back."

I walk quick as I can without running, no running allowed at school. No running, skipping, jumping, talking, laughing, "eyes ahead, single file, hands where they belong."

Mr. Otis's secretary, Mrs. Ramos, smiles nicely at me. "Have a seat, Sunny. I'll buzz Mr. Otis as soon as he's off the phone."

Boy, does Mr. Otis like to talk! That phone call goes on and on and on. The clock ticks past geography.

Miss Fagin sends Jazzy to check on me.

"Tell her I'm still waiting on the principal," I say, and Jazzy leaves. Mrs. Ramos smiles at me.

"Mrs. Ramos," I say.

"Yes, Sunny?"

"Are there any openings for jobs like yours here? My momma needs a job."

Mrs. Ramos purses her lips together. "No," she says kindly, shaking her head. "In fact, we just heard they're laying off another secretary and two aides."

"Oh, I'm sorry to hear that," I say.

The phone rings and Mrs. Ramos goes back to work.

When the clock ticks past history, Miss Fagin

herself comes looking for me. Her face is all pinched up, annoyed, like she thinks I'm trying to sneak time out of her class.

"You'll need to come back later," she says to me. "We're starting a new section in science and you can't afford to miss it."

What does she mean by that? I "can't afford to miss it." Doesn't she know I get straight As? "But, Miss Fagin . . ."

"No buts," she says. "I told you, Mr. Otis is a busy man."

"Maybe try again at recess," Mrs. Ramos suggests.

At recess time, Mr. Otis is out at a meeting.
At lunch, he's on the phone.

At reading time — since I'm a whole five chapters ahead of the class — I ask Miss Fagin, please can I go to the principal's office again. Miss Fagin quizzes me on the chapters to make sure I'm telling the truth. Why would I lie about reading? I love reading! I pass her little test, and finally she lets me go.

Mr. Otis is in another meeting.

"It's with the new superintendent," Mrs. Ramos says. "The top dog." She smiles. "It could be hours."

Jeeesh. Phone calls, meetings, phone calls, meetings, no wonder Mr. Otis is such a grump. No wonder he doesn't smile or have time to learn our names or visit our classroom and read our poems or write more sparkly speeches.

Davina and Crystal are standing in the hallway reading my flier about the Kid's Day meeting.

"Where's the *Community Room*?" Davina says to me, like it's some nasty place.

Crystal looks me up and down, evaluating what I'm wearing like she always does, like she's just looking for something to make fun of.

I look down quick to remember what I'm wearing.

I've got on my striped wool sweater with yellow, green, and red all woven in. It's beautiful. Momma and I bought it at "Sally's Boutique." That's the fun-secret name Momma and I made up for the Salvation Army. The sweater had a designer label and the price tag said it was forty-five dollars marked down to four dollars. And because it was a Wednesday, which is 50-percent-off day at Sally's Boutique, I got it for two dollars!

"It's designer," I say to Crystal. Momma and

I don't care about designer labels, but those bus-girls are always bragging about "designer this and designer that" so I figure this will shut her up.

My mind flashes back to last month, when Davina and Crystal laughed at my jeans with the sewed-on flowers that I wore to Morning Share Time. Davina thought she recognized them as a pair of her old pants her mother gave away to the Salvation Army. She said "Salvation Army" like it was dog-turd, almost too nasty to say. I was so embarrassed to be wearing that mean girl's old thrown-away clothes.

"No way that sweater's designer," Davina says, crossing her arms across her chest.

"It *is* designer," I say. "And the Community Room is at Riverview Towers."

Crystal and Davina squish up their noses like they just smelled that dog-turd again, a big fat *nasty* one.

"Why don't you have the meeting here at school?" Crystal asks. "That way everybody can come."

I'm thinking, *I don't want you to come, please don't come*, but that wouldn't be very deputy mayor–like of me. "Maybe I'll have the March meeting here at school, but today —"

"My mother doesn't want me hanging around the river," Davina says.

Jazzy is by my side now, listening. "Good, then don't come," she says.

"How would we get there after school, any-way?" Crystal says.

"Walk," I say. "It's only five blocks."

"Walk?" Crystal says. "Five blocks? In the city? In *your hood*? No way."

"There's nothing wrong with my neighbor-hood," I say. "And nothing wrong with Riverview Towers. . . ."

"Yeah, right," Davina says. "If you like ghetto."

My brain snaps like an icicle and I slap that girl's face hard.

My heart is pounding. My hand stings. I feel like I'm going to faint.

Davina is bug-eyed shocked. She touches her palm to her cheek.

"Principal's office, now!" Miss Fagin says, grabbing me with one arm and Davina with the other, leading us down the hall.

I am so ashamed. I wish I had a hood-tent I could pull down over my face so people in the hallway wouldn't see it was me, Sunny Holiday, being led along like a criminal.

"I won't have girls fighting like animals," Miss Fagin shouts.

Kids and teachers are staring at us.

"Not on my watch," Miss Fagin rants, her face all red. "This is a place of learning, not some —"

"I didn't do *anything*, Miss Fagin," Davina blurts out, crying. "We were just talking and she hauled off and hit me. Sunny started it. She's always starting trouble."

Miss Fagin stares angry in my eyes. This lady doesn't know me. I bet she's going to take Davina's side. I can't believe I hit that girl. I've never hit anybody in my whole life, not once. It's like my hand just sprung out of my body without my telling it to. *Oh, Mrs. Lullaby, I wish you were here. You know me. You know I'm good.*

Smiling Mrs. Ramos is not at her desk. The door that says *Principal* is cracked open. Mr. Otis is not on the phone, not away at a meeting. He's sitting right there at his desk, punching numbers on a calculator. He scowls and shakes his head at the calculator like he's not happy with its conclusion.

Miss Fagin raps on the door. "Excuse me, Mr. Otis."

Mr. Otis looks up, and Miss Fagin hauls us into his room.

"These two girls were fighting, Mr. Otis," Miss Fagin says, like she's a police officer testifying in court. "I saw this one, Sunny Holiday, slap this one, Davina Bishop, right in the face."

I wilt like a dandelion sprayed with poison.

I've been trying to get Mr. Otis to pay attention to me for a long time.

Well, he's paying attention now.

Now he even knows my name.

Three days suspension. That's my punishment. It's one of Mr. Otis's New Hope "bully-free-zone"

rules. You hit somebody, you're out. No excuses, no exceptions.

Momma has to come pick me up from school.

When I see her face, I finally start crying.

Momma listens to Mr. Otis explain the New Hope bully-free-zone rules and the nature of my crime and punishment. She thanks him for his time and says she is certain this will never happen again.

When we get outside and it's just the two of us, Momma looks me in the eyes.

"Tell me what happened," she says.

I tell her the whole story, exactly as it happened.

Momma lets out a long sigh like a dinosaur breathing out fire, but instead of fire, all that comes out in the cold, cold air is smoke.

"No matter what that awful girl did to provoke you, what you did was *wrong*, Sunny. You know that, right?"

"Yes, Momma." I nod, my head slumping down, staring at the ground.

"But *one mistake* does not make a good person bad," Momma says. "And you are a good person, Sunny, a kind, smart, *good* person. Don't you dare let this one mistake drag you down. Do you hear me?"

"Yes, Momma. I do."

We start walking.

"Well, Momma, one good thing is, Monday's your birthday, and since I can't go to school, I can spend the whole day with you."

"That's after you get your homework done."

"Of course, Momma. I knew that." My heart sinks, remembering my suspension. Me, Sunny

Holiday, straight-A student, suspended from school.

I'm grumped, slumped, bumped, and down-in-the-dumps dumped as we walk home the five freezing blocks to Riverview.

Waiting at a light, Momma lifts my chin and looks into my eyes. Chocolate to chocolate. "I love you, baby."

"Love you, too, Momma."

Momma puts her arm around my shoulder and pulls me in close, and bit by bit it gets warmer.

CHAPTER ELEVEN

The Kid's Day Committee

I think free money is a good idea. Don't you?

"I'm going to cancel the Kid's Day meeting," I say when we reach home.

"Do you think that's the right thing to do?" Momma asks. "You're having lunch with Mayor Little tomorrow. Aren't you supposed to give him a report on how your Kid's Day plans are coming along?"

In addition to planning Kid's Day, Mayor Little

wants me to report on any issues or problems people are having at Riverview Towers. In January, I set up an office.

It's actually not a real office, just a corner of the Community Room with some furniture the mayor sent over, a desk and two chairs — one for me and one for any constituent who comes to chat with me — and a notebook and pen so I can write down their concerns and ideas and questions for the mayor. Oh, and a little glass bowl of lollipops. I saw they had lollipops on the counter in the bank Momma goes to. Pioneer Savings it's called, and I thought that was a sweet idea.

Only two people stopped by my office to talk the first time I opened for business. My office hours are Saturday mornings from ten to eleven.

When I originally set up my deputy mayor headquarters, it didn't seem private enough. Momma and Jo-Jo's friends walking by waving "hey, baby," old folks sitting around staring over at me, people traipsing through with their laundry baskets, babies crawling up into my lap trying to grab the lollipops.

My clever momma fixed that. At Sally's Boutique she bought me a "partition," sort of like a folding wall, three wooden panels that open and close for privacy. Momma painted it my favorite color, yellow, and decorated it with stencils from Crafty Lady. My momma's so good at making old things look new, clothes and furniture and everything. She makes them "Sherry Chic" original.

Now, with a wall, it feels more like a real office.

Thirteen kids show up for my first Kid's Day committee meeting at four o'clock. Jazzy, of course, Kathina, Birdy, and Keisha from our class.

Louis Loomie and Su-Gene from Mrs. Sherman's place. The new boy on fifth, Jay Kwan, along with Jazzy's boyfriend, Eli Stokes.

"He's *not* my boyfriend," Jazzy whispers to me.

"Not yet," I whisper-tease back, "but Valentine's Day is coming."

Ritu and Pradeep Depaki come with a plate of warm pastries their mother made. And, finally, the Levy twins, Brenda and Becky.

Oh, and I almost forgot. Manny Woodson showed up, too. So what.

Momma brings down a jug of apple juice and a huge bowl of hot buttered popcorn. It sure is nice having her home when I get home from school, even though I know how worried she is about finding a job. The newspaper want ads were out on the table again early this morning when I woke up, and just now upstairs I saw all her pages of notes with names of people and companies she's calling. *No luck.*

I thumbtack a poster board to the wall to take notes at our meeting. I've got the fancy new yellow pen Momma bought me with the little silver sun ornament on top. I've decided that even though the Kid's Day holiday was my idea, I'm going to hang low for a while and let my friends share their thoughts first.

Mrs. Lullaby does that when our class is discussing something important, planning a party or a trip. She'll say, "Ideas, people?" and then she'll write what we say on the blackboard. She doesn't compare or judge or question or say anybody's idea is better than anybody else's, she just writes them all down equal.

It feels good to see your idea respected on the board like that.

"Thanks for coming," I say when everyone is seated. "I appreciate your time." Earlier, Jazzy helped me set up folding chairs in a circle. I think a circle works better than a square when you want everybody to be seen and feel important.

"Next January is going to be the first annual Kid's Day holiday here in the city of Riverton," I say. "This committee, all of us, we get to plan it."

"*Yes!*" Eli says, pumping his arm all proud, and everybody laughs.

I smile. This is starting out well. "I thought we could begin by shouting out ideas for what we think our holiday could be like. I'll make a list to share with Mayor Little when I meet with him tomorrow."

"Sunny's meeting with the mayor?" I hear Brenda Levy ask Jazzy.

"Yep. He's sending a limousine to bring her to that fancy Jack's restaurant over in Springtown."

I rap my pen on the candy dish to get their attention. Jazzy mouths "sorry."

"Okay, so, let's think about what we want Kid's Day to be like. Let's use our imaginations and make a really long list. And no judging, okay? Don't worry your idea isn't good. Every idea is a good —"

"Money," Eli shouts, and people laugh.

I write *Money* on the poster.

"What you mean, money?" Manny asks.

"That's what we need for Kid's Day," Eli says. "Money. Lots and lots of money. If we're going to have a good holiday, we gotta do it up right. *Ka-ching, ka-ching.*"

"There should be prizes," Ritu says.

"And music," Jazzy says. "Maybe you can get your friend Candy Wrapper to come, Sunny."

"Sunny knows Candy Wrapper?!" I hear Becky say.

"*Uh-h* —" Jazzy starts, and I give her stare-eyes until she stops. She mouths "sorry" again.

"Let's have good food," Pradeep says, "every kind of treat we want."

I print their ideas on the poster. "Nice job, everybody. What else?"

"Families get to be together," Keisha says quietly, "for the whole day."

Nobody says anything for a while. Everybody knows Keisha's mother got busted for dealing. First-time offense, but by the time she gets out, Keisha will be in high school and her mother still won't have a job to support their family. That's why she started dealing in the first place, for money to pay her bills.

I think about my daddy. I smile kindly at Keisha and she nods at me. Keisha and I share something. We both know what it's like to miss someone in your family who you love so much.

Yeah, I like Keisha's idea. Families ought to be together on Kid's Day, all day long, morning, noon, and night.

"Ice cream," Su-Gene says. "There should be ice cream."

I write that down.

"Nothing special about ice cream," Jay Kwan says.

"No judging," I say. "The more ideas the better."

"Sorry," Jay says. "I got one. How about no homework that day."

"And TV as late as you want," Louis adds.

"With snacks," Birdy says.

"You're all wacked," Eli says, standing up, strutting around. "On *my holiday*, I want money. That's all. Money. Big fat green ones, stacked up high." He raises his hand in the air to show. "Money up to here so I can buy what I want."

Jazzy giggles.

"You're crazy," Manny says. "You think that little mayor's going to . . ."

"It's Mayor Little," I say.

The Levy girls giggle.

"Big, little, whatever," Manny says. "You think that mayor's going to hand out money for free, Eli? You're wacked, man."

"Hey, no judging," Eli says. "You heard Sunny say it herself. Every idea is a good one. I'm just keeping it real. I think free money is a good idea. Don't you?"

And then everybody's talking all at once. . . .

"It's a great idea."

"Show me the money, honey."

"I'll take a hundred."

"A thousand."

"A million."

Oh, no . . .

"Oh, yeah!"

"Uh-huh!"

I rap my yellow pen on the candy dish, but everybody's too excited seeing green to pay attention.

Meeting adjourned.

Later that night, I read over the poster list of ideas.

I write my report for the mayor.

Dear Mayor Little,

The committee to plan the first annual Kid's Day holiday held its first official meeting at Riverview Towers Community Room on February 6. Attendance was good. Fourteen people, counting myself. We all shared our ideas of what we thought Kid's

Day should be like. The ideas were interesting. I think we made a good start.

As an assignment for our next meeting, I asked committee members to talk with at least three other kids — people who aren't in our class and don't live at Riverview, you know, different kids — about what ideas they have for Kid's Day. I think it is important to get diverse perspectives.

We are going to meet again on March 6. This time I think I will hold the meeting at New Hope School so that kids who don't live at Riverview Towers will be able to come, too.

Respectfully submitted,
Sunny Holiday
Junior Deputy Mayor, Riverton, NY

"Does it sound boring?" I ask Momma. "Tell me the truth."

"It's perfect," Momma says. "When a group is first getting together, it is important that you start by trusting one another, respecting one another, and showing you are going to do your part."

"We were doing fine until the money," I say.

"I hear ya, baby," Momma says. "Money can muck up anything."

True, I think, *but our family could sure use some muck.*

CHAPTER TWELVE

Lunch with the Mayor

I'll take that as a compliment.

It's raining on Saturday when I take the elevator to the lobby to wait for the mayor's limousine to pull up. I'm wearing my favorite yellow sweater and my best skirt.

Good thing it's rain and not snow outside. Visiting Day is tomorrow and I don't want us to have a snow accident like last month.

I'm looking forward to that *hmmm-mmm yum-yummy* big lunch at Jack's Oyster House. But today is just an appetizer. The next two days will be even better. Tomorrow, I get to see Daddy. Hooray! Then Monday's Momma's birthday and we'll have the whole day together. That reminds me. I need to buy Momma a present later.

Jazzy isn't coming with me to see Mayor Little this time. She woke up with a sore throat this morning, and Jo-Jo said she had to stay in bed.

"Don't worry, Jazzy," I promised her. "I'll bring you back something good."

❀   ❀   ❀

Downstairs, Mr. Petrofino, the Soup, is shake-shake-shaking rock salt out of a coffee can around the entranceway. Cold air is blowing in around him.

"Watch your step out there today," he says to me. "It's going to be a sheet of ice."

"Oh, I'm not walking," I say, casually, not bragging or anything. "Mayor Little is sending a limousine for me. We have a lunch meeting."

Mr. Petrofino's eyes roll upward. He keeps on shaking salt crystals on the ice. "Tell Rocky that Al Petrofino said hello."

"You know Mayor Little?" I say.

"We went to school together," the Soup says. "A long time ago."

"I was hoping you would come to my office hours a few weeks back, Mr. Petrofino. The mayor wants me to report on any concerns or problems people at Riverview are having."

"It's *my* job to take care of problems around here," the Soup snaps back in a grumpy voice.

"What's Rocky Little going to do for Riverview? He never does anything except talk a good game."

"Maybe he's changing," I say. "Maybe he will listen if I —"

"You think he's going to listen to *you*? He's not going to listen to you. Rocky Little just wants another picture in the paper, showing how he's reaching out to the community, caring about kids. He's just using you to make himself look good."

"That's harsh, Mr. Petrofino. Cynical," I say, feeling hurt for the mayor.

"That's life, Sunny. People use people to get what they want."

A long black limousine pulls up out front with its headlights on, wipers swooshing. Mr. Namesh, the mayor's chauffeur, comes to the door with an umbrella so I won't get rained on. "Good afternoon, Sunny," he says.

"Good afternoon, Mr. Namesh."

"How are you today?" he says.

"Fine, sir, and you?"

"Just fine, thanks. Roads are getting slippery. They say it's going to be bad tonight, worse tomorrow, but we should be fine today."

Outside of Jack's restaurant, Mr. Namesh double-parks the car, lights blinking, and escorts me to the door. Right away I see Mayor Rockefeller Little the Third sitting in his specially reserved red leather booth in the back right-hand corner. He's talking with two men. People are always stopping to talk with the mayor.

A lady offers to take my coat. She hangs it up in a little room and hands me a round tab with a number on it. "Here you go, sweetie."

It's toasty warm in here, and the food smells delicious. My mouth is watering just thinking about that juicy steak I'm going to order and those creamy mashed potatoes and brown-sugar-topped carrots and chocolate layer cake for dessert.

"It's Sunny, right?" a man in a fancy suit says to me.

I think I remember that he owns this place. "That's right, sir. Sunny Holiday."

"Welcome back to Jack's, Sunny Holiday. What a nice name. Have you ever heard of Billie Holiday, the singer?"

"Of course," I say, laughing. "Everybody knows Billie Holiday. Best jazz-blues singer ever."

The man smiles. "She's one of my favorites," he says.

"You should hear my momma," I say. "She sings just like her. I think better, even. Everybody's always telling my momma she should send tapes in to recording studios."

"Does your mother perform locally?" the man asks. "I'm sorry, I should have introduced myself. I'm Brad Rosen, the owner. I've been thinking about offering live jazz on the weekends."

"You mean you could hire my mother?"

Mr. Rosen laughs. "You are charming, Sunny."

"I'll take that as a compliment."

Mr. Rosen laughs harder. "Well, I'd like to hear your mother sing first, but yes, I think if she really does sing as well as you say she does, I would like to hire her. If she sounds like Billie Holiday and is half as charming as you, I think that would be great for business."

"Oh, thank you, Mr. Rosen." I grab his hand and shake it.

Wait till I tell Momma I got a job for her!

The two men who were talking with the mayor pass by us on their way out the door. Mayor Little motions to me to come join him. Mr. Rosen escorts me over.

"I see you've met my little deputy mayor," Mayor Little says in a loud voice, looking around the restaurant as if he wants to make sure the other patrons hear him. "Have a seat, Sunny," he says.

I slide into the red leather booth that's big enough for a family.

"What would you like to drink, Sunny?" Mr. Rosen asks me.

"Orange soda if you have it, please."

Mr. Rosen smiles. "Will cola do?"

"Sure," I say.

"I'll see that we have orange the next time you come," Mr. Rosen says. "Enjoy your lunch." He walks away, then comes back. He hands me a card with his name and telephone number on it. "Have your mother give me a ring."

Whoopee! Just wait till I tell Momma!

A waiter comes and fills my water glass. I spread my napkin just so on my lap. The mayor and I consult our menus and place our orders. He passes me the bread basket, and I put a roll on the little china bread plate next to the silver forks.

"So how's things?" the mayor asks.

"Great," I say. "The Kid's Day planning committee . . ."

Mayor Little looks toward the front door of the restaurant. He flicks up the cuff of his suit jacket to check his watch.

"We had our first meeting yesterday and we've already come up with lots of good —"

"Excuse me for a second," Mayor Little says. He presses a number on his cell phone and puts it to his ear, taking a sip of his drink.

How rude. Just plain rude. I think if you're out to lunch with someone in a restaurant, you ought to concentrate on talking to that person, not be all blabbin' on your phone to somebody else.

"Yeah, I hear the roads are getting bad," the mayor says into the phone. "Maybe you better get over here and take some shots in case the papers don't show up."

I get a suspicious feeling inside. I think about what Mr. Petrofino said.

"Sorry, Sunny," Mayor Little says, flipping his phone shut. "What were you saying?"

"Mr. Petrofino told me to say hello to you."

"Mr. who?"

"Mr. Al Petrofino, the superintendent at Riverview Towers. He said you two went to school together."

"Oh, right," Mayor Little says. "I saw him that night I made my speech over there. How's Al doing these days? Talk about a fall from grace. Poor guy. He was top of our class, corner office, beautiful wife and daughter, and now he's fixing faucets in the ghe —" Mayor Little stops like he got stung by a bee. A gigantic bee. He takes a long sip of water.

"Mayor Little? Were you just going to say *ghetto*?"

The mayor spits and coughs. "No, certainly not!"

"Yes, you were," I say loudly. My whole body is shaking mad.

Mayor Little smiles at two ladies at the next table who are staring at us.

"You misunderstood me, Sunny," he says in a low voice.

"Oh, no, I didn't. I didn't misunderstand a thing." I slide my butt across that fine red leather seat, set my boots on the floor, and stand tall. "I heard you plain as a fire siren."

Someone behind me clears his throat. A tall, tall handsome black man. "Mayor Little," the man says with a nod. He has a distinguished accent, African.

"Superintendent," the mayor says, sliding around the booth to stand and shake the tall man's hand.

The mayor hardly ever stands. This brother must be important.

"Sunny," the mayor says, nodding his head sly-sweetly at me like *be good now, okay?* "Allow me to introduce the new superintendent of Riverton Schools, Mr. Michael Ogunyase."

Superintendent. I remember what Mrs. Ramos said that day in Mr. Otis's office. A firefly flies into my head and spark, spark, sparks.

"Are you the top dog over all the teachers and all the principals of all the schools?" I say.

Mr. Ogunyase smiles. "Yes, I guess you might say I am."

Spark, spark, spark, spark, spark.

"Mayor Little," I say in a charming voice, "would it be all right if the superintendent joined us for lunch?"

The mayor is so happy to be free from squirm-dangling like an old fish on a hook about that word he said, he nearly dances. "Certainly, Sunny. Wonderful idea." Mayor Little is all smiles now. "Please, Michael, won't you join us?"

Through the salad course, and the steak course, and the chocolate-cake-and-tea course, I give that nice superintendent an earful about how Mrs. Lullaby is the most wonderful teacher ever and how she collects our worries in her silver suitcase and how she brings out the best in us because she believes in us and when someone believes in you that much, you just cannot let them down, you work harder and harder, and get smarter and smarter. . . .

"You're a smooth negotiator, Sunny," Mayor Little says to me as we are leaving.

"I'll take that as a compliment, sir."

I'm so happy about telling Mr. Ogunyase about Mrs. Lullaby and hopefully getting her job back that I almost let the mayor slide on his ghetto bad. Then, just as we part, I say, "Mr. Mayor?"

"Yes, Sunny?" He turns, flicking up a big blue umbrella over his head.

I wait until he looks at me. "I've got excellent hearing, sir." I stare-eye the mayor good until he catches my meaning.

Mayor Little nods.

"But I'm also good at giving second chances if a person owns up to his mistake."

The mayor purses his lips and nods. "Thank you, Sunny."

"How was your lunch?" Mr. Namesh asks. He takes my arm so I won't slip as he helps me back into the limousine. The sidewalk is a skating rink.

"Fantastic," I say.

Mr. Namesh closes my door. I set my leftover bags next to me and I sink into the thick, soft, cushy leather seat. Maybe someday I'll have a car like this. I lean my head back, feels like a pillow, and close my eyes, pretending I'm Candy Wrapper. I start humming one of her songs.

Mr. Namesh asks if the heat is all right.

"Yes, sir, thank you."

I notice Mr. Namesh put a bottle of water in the holder for me. That was thoughtful of him.

"It was a very good meeting," I say. "I got my momma a new job. I maybe got my teacher back her old job. I got a doggy bag for me and Jazzy and a kitty bag for our cats. And the mayor and I had a good talk."

Mr. Namesh smiles at me in his rearview mirror. "Nice work," he says, and then turns his eyes right back to the road.

I notice that he is driving very slowly, cautiously.

"Thank you," I say. "You do nice work yourself, Mr. Namesh."

When I get home, I remember I need to go shopping for Momma's birthday present. It's too nasty-slippery outside to walk to Daisy's or Crafty Lady. Good thing it's just ice, not snow. Ice melts. We'll be fine to drive tomorrow.

But what to get for Momma?

I wait a while and then it comes to me. I know! I'll make Momma a card and surprise her with the news about the singing job at Jack's. That means keeping the job a secret all the way until Monday, but I can do that for Momma.

I fold a piece of yellow construction paper. On the front I draw a picture of a lady with a microphone. I make a little air bubble and print *I've got you under my skin* — that's one of Momma's favorite jazz recordings. Inside I write:

Dear Momma,

    Wear your prettiest skirt and your prettiest blouse when you perform at Jack's Oyster House.
The owner, Mr. Rosen, wants to hire you to sing!!
He gave us this card and said give him a ring.
        Happy, happy birthday, Momma,
        Love,
            Sunny ☺

Momma is going to love this present! She always says, "I don't need a present. Just make me a card for my birthday." Wait until she reads this! I can just hear her shrieking all happy and then rushing upstairs to tell Jo-Jo.

Before I go to bed, I lay out my clothes for Visiting Day tomorrow. I look over the Valentines I made for Daddy. He's going to love them. I can't wait to see him!

I say my gratitudes. "Dear God, thank you for: Momma, Daddy, Jazzy, Mr. Namesh, Mr. Rosen, Billie Holiday, firefly ideas, Mr. Ogunyase, the food at Jack's, and birthday card surprises." I turn off the light.

"P.S. Please don't let it snow tomorrow."

CHAPTER THIRTEEN

God Sends an Angel

I know my daddy's name.

When I wake up early Sunday morning all excited, I know right away for certain something's wrong. The little numbers aren't glowing on my alarm clock, the light's not on in the hallway, I don't hear Momma singing in the kitchen, I don't smell breakfast, and it's cold, really cold, freezing Eskimo Alaska igloo cold.

Visiting Day, oh, no!!

Brrrrrrrrrrr, I shiver from head to toes. I feel around in the dark for my slippers and bathrobe. I walk with my hand touching the hallway wall so I won't trip. "Momma?"

"Out here, Sunny."

Momma is sitting at the table with two tall dinner candles lit. Her eyelids are low and her face droops down like she didn't sleep well last night.

"The power's out," she says. "It's been out since two A.M. or so."

But it's Visiting Day. My heart beats quicker. "What time is it now?"

Momma looks at her watch. "Six o'clock." She tries a smile. "Maybe you want to jump back in bed where it's warmer. I've been listening to the radio on and off, good thing I had batteries, and they're saying the ice is so heavy it's knocking down trees, pulling down lines, thousands of people are without power and . . ."

"What about the roads?"

"A sheet of ice."

"But we're still going, right?"

Momma closes her eyes.

"Momma." I move toward her. "We're still going to visit Daddy, right?"

"I'm sorry, Sunny."

"NO, Momma. We're going. We have to go."

"We can't, baby. The roads are too dangerous. There are tree limbs down —"

"Come on, Momma, *please*. What if you drive really, really slow, like ten miles an hour or something?"

"Not in Mrs. Gordon's ship, Sunny. It's not our car."

"But, Momma —"

"Sunny, stop." Momma bursts out crying. "I'm sorry, Sunny. I miss him, too. I'm scared, honey. What if I don't get a job, what if he doesn't get parole, and now this . . . this . . . *storm* is just, just *icing on the cake.*" She clamps her hand over her mouth and turns away.

I rush to give her a hug.

"Icing on a birthday cake, Momma?"

She laughs and I laugh, too. I rub her shoulders.

"This is wrong," Momma says, turning away. "I don't mean to put this on you, baby."

"It's okay, Momma," I say. "You don't always have to be so brave and strong. I know how hard it is. Taking care of me all by yourself, trying to find work, studying for school."

Momma looks so sad, like that little bump in the road just turned into a big old crater-size pothole.

"Guess what, Momma." I know what will cheer her up. "I have a birthday surprise for you!"

"What's that?" she asks, wiping the tears off her cheeks with the sleeve of her bathrobe.

I take a candle and walk to my room, get her card, and come back. "Here, Momma, happy-happy birthday."

Momma reads her present and smiles a sunny smile so bright it could melt all that ice outside and then some.

"Where did you come from, Sunny?"

"From you, Momma. You and Daddy."

Just saying the name *Daddy* makes my heart crack open. Tears rise inside me and spout out of my eyes like lava from a volcano. I cry and cry and cry. *Oh, Daddy, I miss you so much. I want to see you. I need to see you.*

Momma hugs me. I open my eyes. I see our wall book over there, all dim in the candlelight.

All those good things. Oh, please, God, send us a good thing now. Momma and I need an angel right now this minute.

Nothing happens.

"Let's go snuggle for a while," Momma says.

We curl up like kittens on the couch under blankets. Queen Jadie leaps up on Momma's back. Group snug. Soon we're all fast asleep.

Knock-knock-knock-knock-knock.

I open my eyes. It's light outside. Someone's at our door.

"Wonder who that is?" Momma says, wiping her eyes and yawning.

"An angel," I say.

Now, some people might think an angel comes in a long white flowy gown, with a golden halo and wings.

Not ours. Our angel came in a long thick yellow jacket, with a helmet and shiny black boots. And a silver badge.

RFD. Riverton Fire Department.

Momma's best girlfriend, Jo-Jo, woke up early this morning, too, and saw the situation outside and remembered it was Visiting Day. She got herself dressed and walked straight up to the sixth floor and asked Chief Slade if he would please drive Momma and me to Mount Burden. That's what true friends do. They don't say "call if you need me." They do what you need.

A fire truck is a powerful good thing.

Chief Slade buckles me tight into the seat up front next to him. Momma gets in behind us. We're on top of the world above the highway.

When a slow van gets in our way, the chief lets me flip the switch for the siren. *Ooo-whee*, that was fun.

When we reach Mount Burden Correctional Facility, Momma and I wait in line with the other visitors to go through security. The guard checks through Momma's pocketbook. He smiles at my Valentines and slides them back into the envelope. We walk through the metal detector. A loud buzzer buzzes and the steel doors crank open. We're almost there.

In the visiting room, Momma and I go to the vending machines and buy Daddy a can of soda, a bag of chips, and a candy bar. Momma gives our purchases to a guard and tells him these are for Hercules Holiday. The guard checks his clipboard and makes a note. Inmates can't take food treats back to their cells, but they can enjoy them while they're talking with their visitors.

Momma and I sit in orange plastic chairs with all the other families waiting. I stare through the thick plastic window-wall to the door that Daddy will be coming out of soon. I can't wait to see his face!

When it's time, Momma and I will sit in a little cubicle on one side of the window-wall and Daddy will sit on the other side. We won't be able to hug or kiss or touch hands, even, but we'll be able to talk over phones and study each other's faces for a whole long hour.

There's a lady next to me holding a little boy on her lap. The lady looks so beaten-down sad and far away. The little boy is kicking his legs against the lady, fidgeting. There's no place for him to play. There aren't any toys anywhere, and that concrete floor is cold as a sidewalk.

I check the black-and-white clock. Two more minutes.

"No," the little boy screams, "let me down." He's wriggling back and forth good now, his red face all frustrated mad. I wish I had a book to read him or one of my deputy mayor lollipops. I tap his arm. I smile at him. I bop my head back and forth and stick my tongue out and make my eyes all crazy like a clown. The boy giggles. The lady's eyes smile *thank you* to me.

I check the clock. One more minute.

I stare through that window-wall, waiting, waiting, staring at that door.

Finally, the door opens and the inmates start to file out. One man after another.

No, no, no, no, no, no . . .

Yes.

"Daddy!" I shout. Momma and I stand up.

A guard hands Daddy the vending machine treats we bought him and points to cubicle number six. Momma and I rush over to the number six spot on our side of the window. We sit on the metal stools.

Daddy's walking toward us, smiling. He's wearing blue pants and a shirt with his number on it. 00825-478.

That's one of the ice-cold hard things I learned the first time we visited Daddy here. In prison you're a number, not a name.

I know my daddy's name. Hercules. Hercules Holiday. My daddy's a good daddy, a great artist. My daddy's a hero, a giant.

Momma picks up the orange phone on our side and hands it to me. Only one of us can talk at a time. "You first, baby."

I put the receiver to my ear, getting my mouth ready to talk.

Tears are streaming down Daddy's beautiful black face. He puts his palm against the window-wall. I do the same on my side. Daddy's big strong hand blooms out around my little one. He smiles so sweetly, his brown eyes glimmering.

Daddy talks into his phone. "How's my baby girl?"

"Perfect, Daddy," I say. "I got you and Momma both right here."

CHAPTER FOURTEEN

Sunny's Restaurant

Icing on the cake.

The next morning when I wake up, it's dark and cold. The power's still out.

I lie in bed thinking about how good it was to finally see my daddy and how good it was of Jo-Jo to tell Chief Slade what we needed and how good it was of Chief Slade to drive us all the way to Mount Burden and back.

On the way home last night, I let Momma take the front seat. I heard her asking the chief about himself, where he was from and all. The chief told Momma he's got two younger sisters he's putting through college. Imagine! That explains why he's living at Riverview Towers and not up on Hill Street in a fancy house. He put his little sisters before himself. I wish Momma had a big brother who could help her out with tuition.

It's Momma's birthday!

Maybe I can make her breakfast somehow.

I flick on my flashlight. I layer two heavy sweaters over my bathrobe, slip on another pair of socks and a thick wool hat. I'm bundled up pudgy as a polar bear.

Momma is still sleeping. Good.

I open the refrigerator and use my flashlight to find the orange juice and milk, closing the door quick to keep the cold in. We don't know how long the power will be out. I take down a box of graham crackers and a jar of peanut butter. I set out two plates. I spread peanut butter on two big crackers. I slice a banana and use two circles for eyes, one for a nose, and then a curved slice for a smile on each cracker. I stick a raisin in the center of each banana-eye. I stick a whole bunch of raisins on for hair. I smile. Funny people.

I take two fancy glasses out of the china closet, the kind Momma and Daddy have champagne in on New Year's Eve. I pour us each a glass of juice.

I pull the dead leaves off the poinsettia to spruce it up. I light more candles. I sit on the couch with Queen Jade, snuggled under some blankets, and wait.

When Momma comes out of her room, I say, "Surprise! Happy birthday, Momma. Welcome to Sunny's Restaurant."

"You made me breakfast, Sunny? Oh, thank you, honey. How nice."

In honor of the special occasion, Momma lets Queen Jade sit on the table by us while we're eating. That is never, ever allowed.

"It's your lucky day," I say to Queen Jadie.

"No," Momma says, "it's mine."

Later, Momma sings some of her favorite Billie Holiday recordings — "God Bless the Child," that's her favorite, and "Easy to Love" and "Them There Eyes" and "A Fine Romance."

Momma starts "I've Got My Love to Keep Me Warm."

"Come on, baby, sing it with me," she says.

Momma snaps her fingers and moves to the music. I join in.

> *"The snow is snowing*
> *The wind is blowing*
> *But I can weather the storm.*
> *What do I care how much it may storm?*
> *I've got my love to keep me warm."*

When we get to the part about icicles forming, Momma shrugs her shoulders and smiles, and we belt it out bright as we can:

> *"What do I care if icicles form?*
> *I've got my love to keep me warm."*

"Breakfast was delicious, Sunny," Momma says. "And singing with you was icing on the cake."

CHAPTER FIFTEEN

A New Day

I love how you see the world, Sunny.

We get our heat and lights back on late Monday afternoon. Good thing. Momma and I are so happy to see those orange and white American Grid trucks outside with their bright lights swirling and the workers in hard hats fixing the wires, we almost run out and hug them.

New Hope is closed Monday because of the storm and so I only have to miss two real days of class due to my suspension. Jazzy is going to bring me my assignments, and I plan on reading at least two of my "your-choice" books from the library.

On Tuesday, Momma and I take a long walk. In addition to the nine's-fine, f-and-g's resolution, Momma insists we get exercise every day. We go to Sally's Boutique and each get a dress for the Valentine's Girls' Night party Saturday night. Then we get some red feathers and silver sequins at Crafty Lady so that Momma can make our new dresses Sherry Chic original. We walk quickly past Mid-Nite's Bar and Grill where there was a shooting last year. "Stay away from there, do you hear me?" Momma reminds me like always. We get some candy at Mrs. Milo's store.

Heading home, I tell Momma about street shells. She scrunches her eyes and looks down.

She gets a big smile on her face. "I love how you see the world, Sunny."

When we pass the bus house, a big city bus stops. The door swooshes open and out comes the red-hooded boy from the other day.

He looks at me. "What up, famous?"

Momma grabs my hand.

"My name is Sunny," I say. "What's yours?"

He shrugs his shoulders.

"What school do you go to?" I ask.

"Done with that," he says.

"Sunny?" Momma whispers, squeezing my hand.

"How old are you?" I say to the boy.

"Sixteen."

"And you already graduated high school?"

"No," he says. "I told you. I'm done with that. What's school gonna do for me?"

"It's going to get you into college," I say.

"Sunny," Momma says. "Do you know this boy?"

"Not exactly," I say.

The boy walks off.

"Hey," I shout. "What's *your* name?"

"Merry Christmas."

"Say what?" I shout to him. "I said, what's your name?"

"I told you. Merry Christmas. Merry Christmas Calvary."

On Wednesday, Momma and I take the bus to Springtown. We hardly ever do this. We see a matinee movie using the gift certificate Jazzy and Jo-Jo gave us for Christmas. Momma packed popcorn and two juice boxes from home in her pocketbook so we wouldn't have to pay those crazy movie theater prices. My momma's so smart like that.

After the movie, heading toward the museum, we pass by the Crowne Plaza.

"Do you want to go in?" I say.

"No," Momma says. "This is our time. How often do we get to spend a whole nice long beautiful day together? Let alone two in a row!"

When we come out of the museum, we sit on a bench to rest. Momma hands me some crackers and I toss crumbs to the pigeons. We keep walking.

"Let's stop in here," Momma says.

It's an art gallery. The owner herself is there. Momma and I admire the paintings and photographs hung on the walls.

"Do you let other artists hang their stuff in here, too?" I ask. She says yes.

I tell her about my daddy and she gives me her card. "Have him come show me his portfolio," she says.

Momma and I stop in a diner for hot chocolate. Momma asks if I want a piece of pie or something and I say no thanks. Money is tight, and besides, the chocolate is sweet enough for me.

Before we take the bus back, we stop by the statue of Dr. King. Momma takes my hand and we close our eyes and say our own private gratitudes.

On Thursday morning, I wake up with a bad batch of butterflies in my stomach. Momma makes her famous banana muffins for me. She walks me in to school early. Jazzy said she understood and she'd see me there in a while.

The closer Momma and I get to school, the

more my throat starts squeezing up, and my stomach flips and flops, and I wish I hadn't eaten a second banana muffin.

"Are you okay?" Momma asks.

"Yep."

She squeezes my hand.

When Momma and I reach New Hope, we're so early that some of the teachers are still walking up the steps. Mr. Otis is already at his post.

Momma gives me a kiss. She looks in my eyes. "Listen, girl. You made a mistake. You admitted it. You took your punishment. You won't ever do it again. Today's a new day. Okay?"

I nod my head.

"You be respectful to Miss Fagin and Mr. Otis. Stay away from those nasty bus-girls. Be the strong, smart, gonna-be-president-someday girl you *know* you are."

"Yes, Momma."

I watch her walk away. My stomach starts flip-flopping again. My head is hurting. I'm so cold it's like I swallowed a whole frozen river full of icicles.

A new day.

Okay.

I start up the steps.

When I reach the top, Mr. Otis looks at me. Right in my eyes. Eyes-to-eyes.

"Good morning, Sunny," he says.

"Good morning, Mr. Otis." I smile. He said my name!

"May I have a word with you in my office?" he says.

"Sure." *Oh, no. Now what?*

I follow Mr. Otis into his office. He offers me

a seat. He closes the door. He clears his throat. "I, *ugh, hmm, hmm*, wanted to tell you that the New York State test scores for New Hope came in yesterday."

My heart is pounding.

"And your fourth-grade class scored among the smartest fourth graders in the state."

"YES!!" I shout.

"And I had a visit from Superintendent Ogunyase yesterday as well."

Uh-oh, here it comes. *Please, please, please*, let it be so.

"And while I have reservations about Mrs. Lullaby's somewhat unorthodox teaching methods . . ."

"Her method is love," I blurt out. "What's wrong with that?"

Mr. Otis nods his head. He's thinking about that.

"So is she back?" I say, shaking.

"Why don't you see for yourself," Mr. Otis says.

I run, and I mean *run — who cares about rules —* down the hall.

When I turn the corner toward my classroom, I see our door is open.

Will she be there? Please, please, let her be there.

I get to the doorway, then stop, scared in case it isn't true.

I close my eyes and open them.

The silver suitcase is on the desk.

She's reading the laundry on the line.

"MRS. LULLABY!"

I run to hug her, and she scoops me up in her arms.

"Oh, Sunny, how I've missed you," she says.

CHAPTER SIXTEEN

Heart-Sparks and Valentines

Heart-spark. Pass it on.

On Valentine's Day morning, I go to Mr. Petrofino's apartment and ring the door.

"Here," I say, handing back his container, this time filled with pink-frosted cupcakes. "Momma made these this morning. We thought you might enjoy some. Oh, and you don't need to bring us back anything, but I wouldn't mind if you did. You are a *really* good cook, Mr. P."

The Soup smiles.

I quick stick a heart-spark sticker on his shirt. "Heart-spark, pass it on."

He looks down at the sticker. "What's this?" He touches it.

"A new tradition I'm starting for Valentine's Day," I say. "You got heart-sparked. Pass it on."

"What's that mean?" he says.

I hesitate. I'm not sure how to explain. Grumps, slumps, bumps, and dumps. Conversation hearts. Words that matter. Everybody's little light inside. All of a sudden my ideas seems all muddled up and stupid. I stare at the red heart sticker with the street-shell glued-on spark. I look down at my shoes. What a stupid idea.

"I know," Mr. Petrofino says.

I look up.

Mr. Petrofino is nodding his head. "You mean you did something kind for me and now I have to pass it on . . . do something nice for some-body else."

I smile. "That's exactly right, Mr. Petrofino. You have excellent holiday-improvement sense. Maybe you'd like to come to my next meeting to plan the new Kid's Day holiday we're going to have."

"Well," the Soup says, looking serious again. "I am a very busy man, but if I'm available that day, I will try to come."

I turn to leave and then remember. "Oh, wait. We're having a Valentine's dance for the building tonight at the Fines' apartment, 4-C, seven o'clock. I hope you'll come."

Next, I ring Miss Fontenot's bell. No answer. I hear sounds inside. I ring the bell again. No answer. I ring it again, holding the buzzer in longer.

The door opens a crack. She recognizes me. "Yes, Sunny?"

"I have something for you," I say.

Miss Fontenot slides back the chain and opens the door.

"Heart-spark, pass it on," I say, sticking the heart on the shoulder of her bathrobe.

Startled, Miss Fontenot reaches up and pulls the sticker off to look. She holds the heart up close to her eye. Maybe she sees her face in that tiny silver mirror. She sticks the heart-spark back on her bathrobe, this time right over her heart. She pats it good to make sure it stays on. She smiles. She looks younger. She turns and lifts her arm up, then the other arm. She sweeps around the room, light as if she's dancing on air.

"Miss Fontenot," I call over to her. "We're having a Valentine's party tonight at my friend Jazzy Fine's apartment, 4-C, at seven o'clock. We really want you to come and dance."

Miss Fontenot stops swirling. She stares at me. She shakes her head no. Then her head perks up. "Will Claude be there?" she says.

"Who?" I say.

She looks confused. Sad. She moves to shoo me out the door.

"Maybe he'll be there," I say. "Lots of people are coming. Please come. You got heart-sparked. You've got to pass it on."

At three o'clock, I put on my coat and walk down to the bus house. This was right around the time when Merry Christmas Calvary, what a name, got off the bus before.

I wait for a half hour. Three buses stop and unload and pull away. He doesn't come. I'll have to save his sticker for when I see him again.

It's Girls' Night. Valentine's night. Jazzy and Jo-Jo have the lights turned down low with candles lit all around the room. It looks so Hollywood-romantic in here.

Jazz is playing. *"All of me. Why not take all of me. . . ."*

"Woo-hoo, glamorous," Jo-Jo says when she sees me and Momma in our new fancy dresses.

Jo-Jo looks like a movie star herself in a

short-short gold dress with a red feather boa around her neck.

"Never mind us. You are looking *hot* tonight," Momma says. "You are on fire, girl. Somebody better call a fireman. No, wait, a fire *chief!*"

"*Shush,*" Jo-Jo says, and she and Momma nearly topple to the floor laughing.

"Hey, baby," Jazzy's grandma says, hugging me. "I'm so glad you got to see your daddy this time. I prayed hard all last week."

"Thank you, Sister Queen. Your prayers sure worked."

❀   ❀   ❀

This month instead of pizza — we usually always have pizza with different toppings on Girls' Night, depending on what country we're traveling to in our imaginations — Jo-Jo melted a big pot of cheese and a big pot of chocolate. There are plates of different kinds of food to dip into the pots using long silver skewers.

"The cheese one's dinner stuff and the chocolate is dessert," Jo-Jo says.

I stab a small hunk of broiled steak, dip it into the cheese, let it cool off, and take a bite. *"Hmm . . . yumm*, this is delicious."

"It's called fondue," Jazzy says. "Momma said Valentine's night called for something fancy."

I cheese-coat a piece of chicken next, then a mushroom, some broccoli, a grape tomato. For dessert, I dip a strawberry into the warm melted chocolate. Jazzy dips one, too. We both agree that fresh chocolate-covered strawberries beat old boxed chocolates any day.

Chief Slade comes with a bouquet of flowers and Jo-Jo is very happy.

Eli comes with a bag of potato chips and Jazzy is very happy.

Manny Woodson does not come. So what. Who cares.

The doorbell rings.

Mr. Petrofino. He's wearing a black suit, white shirt, red tie, and red silk handkerchief folded in the top pocket of his jacket. There's something on his lapel.

The heart-spark sticker.

The doorbell rings.

Miss Fontenot. She has her heart-spark sticker stuck on her forehead. She's wearing a pretty pink dress. When she sees the fondue, her eyes glisten. "Thank you for bringing me back to Paris, Claude," she says to Mr. Petrofino.

The Soup doesn't ask her what the heck she's talking about.

A slow song comes on.

Miss Fontenot smiles at Mr. Petrofino like he's somebody she knew, somebody she loved, a long long time ago.

Mr. Petrofino steps forward and holds out his arm to Miss Fontenot. "May I have this dance?" he says.

"Well, look at that," Momma whispers to me. "Mr. Petrofino can cook and he can dance, too. That man would be a fine catch."

I see Momma's pretty face in the candlelight. She looks like she's far away. Most likely three hours by ship or fire truck away, picturing her man in prison.

I take a sticker from my pocket.

"Heart-spark. Pass it on," I say, putting the heart on Momma's dress.

"What's this?" she says, smiling.

I explain as best I can.

The next thing I know, Momma's holding a spoon in her hand, pretending it's a microphone. She's singing "My Funny Valentine," except Momma is changing the words. . . .

"My Sunny Valentine,
Sweet sunny valentine,
You are my favorite work of art. . . ."

When the party ends, Momma and I walk up the fire-escape stairs to the roof, our Saturday night tradition. Momma pushes open the door. The wind whooshes a cold *hello*. We pull our coat collars up around our necks and step out onto the beach. We call it the beach because on the Fourth of July and other special summer nights we lie here and look up at the fireworks shooting over to us from Springtown.

I look down at the tar beach. Nothing.

I look up at the tar sky. Diamonds.

Diamonds and stars and planets and galaxies, the moon and who knows beyond.

"It's so bright tonight we need sunglasses," Momma says, and we hug each other laughing.

We don't say anything for a while. Our eyes are closed, making wishes.

"Heart-spark, pass it on," Momma says. "Where'd you get that idea from?"

"It flit in my head like a firefly, and I caught it on paper like in a mayonnaise jar."

"*Hmm-hmmm,*" Momma says. "*Heart-spark, pass it on.* You caught something fine there, girl. Street shells . . . heart-sparks . . . so many good ideas."

"Thanks, Momma."

"You know, Sunny, I think you've only just begun catching all the fireflies coming your way. We better start putting mayonnaise on *everything* — cereal, hot dogs, cupcakes, meatballs — breakfast, lunch, and dinner, so we'll have enough jars for you."

"All I need is a pen and paper."

We laugh. The wind whistles. Momma hugs me for a long, long time.

Tonight I have so many gratitudes I have to haul out my toes, too.

Acknowledgments

With heartfelt thanks to:

My wonderful editor, Jennifer Rees, who hears Sunny's voice like I do, and David Levithan, and everyone at Scholastic Press, Book Clubs, and Book Fairs.

My A+ agents, Tracey and Josh Adams of Adams Literary.

My gifted friend, teacher, and photographer Maureen Goldman, for her inspiring photo of the dandelion in winter, and her phenomenally smart and talented students, especially Miss Jala Moore, for sharing their thoughts about Sunny.

To Selwyn, for filling in the missing pieces.

And always and forever, my wonderful sons, my suns, Dylan, Connor, and Chris. I am so very proud of you.

Heart-spark, pass it on.

Find your light and let it glow.

Bloom like a dandelion. *Bloom, bloom, bloom.*

Till soon, dear readers,

Coleen ☺

About the Author

Coleen Murtagh Paratore is the author of the acclaimed The Wedding Planner's Daughter series as well as *The Funeral Director's Son* and *Mack McGinn's Big Win* and several picture books. The mother of three teenage sons, she lives in upstate New York and on Cape Cod, Massachusetts. Visit Coleen online at www.coleenparatore.com.